EARTH SHATTERING

"The quake—it's coming," Tom warned. "Brace yourselves!"

As Tom was tossed about, an awful roaring sound filled his ears. Then came a loud crack as the ground in front of him ripped apart and a huge opening appeared.

"Run!" Tom screamed to the people near the fissure.

Tom got to his feet but was knocked down again by Dan, who was sliding out of control toward the crack in the earth. As Dan passed him, Tom grabbed his hand. Dan stopped a foot short of the crevice.

"Hold on, Dan!" Tom shouted over the roaring of the earth. "Don't let go!"

The ground heaved again. Shrubs and picnic coolers tumbled past them to pitch into the yawning hole. Tom's feet lost their grip, and Dan's weight began pulling them both inexorably toward the open fissure.

Books in the Tom Swift® Series

A Hardy Boys & Tom Swift Ultra Thriller™

TIME BOMB

Available from ARCHWAY Paperbacks

TOM SWIFT

12

DEATH QUAKE

VICTOR APPLETON

AN ARCHWAY PAPERBACK
Published by POCKET BOOKS
New York London Toronto Sydney Tokyo Singapore

AN ARCHWAY PAPERBACK *Original*

An Archway Paperback published by
POCKET BOOKS, a division of Simon & Schuster Inc.
1230 Avenue of the Americas, New York, NY 10020

Copyright © 1993 by Simon & Schuster Inc.

Produced by Byron Preiss Visual Publications, Inc.

ISBN: 0-671-79529-5

First Archway Paperback printing February 1993

10 9 8 7 6 5 4 3 2 1

TOM SWIFT, AN ARCHWAY PAPERBACK and colophon are registered trademarks of Simon & Schuster Inc.

Cover art by Michael Herring

Printed in the U.S.A.

IL 6+

1

RICK CANTWELL STARED AT THE ELECTRONIC lock on the door to Tom Swift's laboratory. The lock stared back at him with an unblinking red eye.

"Come on, Rick, answer the question, or we'll never get into the lab," said Tom Swift's sister, Sandra.

"Yeah, Rick," Dan Coster chimed in. "Tell the door lock the name of the rock band with the one-armed drummer, or we'll never get Tom out of the lab and onto the beach."

"I don't understand," said Dan's date, Lisa Singleton. "We have to answer a trivia question to get into the laboratory?"

"*We* don't," Sandra explained. "Rick does. He's one of only four people who can let

1

themselves into Tom's lab. And he's hopeless at rock trivia."

"So answer the question, Rick," Mandy Coster said. "I'd like to go on this picnic *today*."

"Okay, then, I'll guess Van Halen," Rick said into the door's audio receptor. "But it doesn't matter if that's the right answer. The lock just wants to match my voiceprint with the one in its memory." As Tom Swift's best friend, Rick had free access to the lab and went there frequently to spend time with Tom and help test his inventions.

The red light blinked out. The door clicked and swung open.

"It's a good thing the answer doesn't matter," said Mandy's cousin, Dan. "You totally blew that one. Any moron knows the group is Def Leppard."

"It's better this way," Mandy said, leading the way through the door. "If Rick had to answer the question correctly, we'd never get in." She stopped suddenly and gasped at the sight of Tom, his head encased in a device of wires and electronic components, lying on his back on the floor, his arms and legs waving in the air.

"Tom, what's wrong?" Mandy hurried toward him, but Sandra grabbed her by the arm.

"Wait. I think he's all right. Look over there."

A large black cat, wearing a smaller version of the electronic headgear, was rolling playfully on the laboratory floor a few feet from Tom, mimicking Tom's motions exactly. Tom and the cat rolled left, then right, and then both kicked their legs into the air.

"This has got to be the weirdest Tom Swift experiment yet," Dan said, shaking his head.

"You mean he does this kind of thing all the time?" Lisa asked, looking doubtful.

"Oh, there's never a dull moment here at Swift Enterprises," Sandra told her. "Between Dad and Tom, there's always some kind of exotic and exciting scientific research going on. But I have to agree with Dan—this one's pretty weird, all right."

As Tom and the cat sat up, Tom noticed his friends and waved them toward a workbench near the door. Then he placed a saucer of milk in front of the cat and closed his eyes in concentration.

The cat padded over to the bowl, and Tom pantomimed its movements, creeping on all fours toward a spot near the cat. When the cat put its head down to drink, Tom lowered his own head toward the floor. As the cat lapped up the milk, Tom seemed to be lapping invisible milk from an invisible bowl in front of him.

"Why didn't I bring my camera?" Rick exclaimed, roaring with laughter. "This has to be the funniest thing I've ever seen!"

3

Just then Rick bumped the workbench and knocked over a canister, which fell to the floor with a loud metallic clank.

Tom opened his eyes, his concentration broken, and stood up. "Hi, there," he called to his friends. He removed the headset and ran his fingers carelessly through his blond hair. "Are we still on for the beach picnic?"

"Sure." Mandy laughed. "Just as soon as you explain why you were crawling on the floor and drinking milk like a cat."

Tom picked up the cat and removed its headset, then scratched it behind the ears. The cat purred in contentment. "I borrowed Mickey here from Mary Ann Jennings, the receptionist at Swift Enterprises. Oh, and that reminds me, Sandra. Don't let me leave today without taking him back to her. His carrier is over there in the corner."

"Okay, Tom."

"You see, Mickey has been helping me put the finishing touches on my psychotronic translator."

"Psycho what? What's that?" Dan asked him.

"It's a device I've been working on to study thought patterns. One participant wears one of these headsets, which contains a transmitter, and the other wears the one with the receiver. The receiver picks up and reads brain-wave activity from the brain's language and conceptual centers. You might say the receiver

4

reads whatever thoughts are uppermost in a person's mind."

"So the cat was reading your mind," Rick said. "You were telling it to roll on the floor and drink the milk, right?"

"No, the device is a translator," Mandy said. "I think Tom's trying to learn cat language."

"Or teach the cat English," Sandra offered.

"Rick was the closest," Tom said. "But it was Mickey who was giving *me* orders. He was wearing the transmitter set, and I was wearing the receiver. I guess I'd better make a note to myself to fine-tune the kinetic input so that the person wearing the receiver won't actually act out the impulses he or she is receiving. It'll be a lot less embarrassing that way."

Tom set the cat down on the workbench and scribbled some notes in his lab book. Mickey paced the top of the workbench restlessly for a moment, then jumped down and began meowing loudly.

"I wonder what's wrong with him?" Lisa said.

"I think he just wants to get back to Mary Ann," Tom said. "It's all right, boy—we'll be out of here in a few minutes."

"I hope so," Dan said. "The summer's half over, you know—there's no time to waste."

"Oh, my gosh!" Lisa exclaimed, eyes wide. "What is that thing?" She ran to hide behind Dan. A seven-foot-tall metal man with glowing red eyes was moving from the rear of the lab toward Tom. "Tom, look out!" Lisa screamed.

Tom looked up. The robot extended one enormous fist in Tom's direction. "Here's that new batch of processors, boss," it said, placing a handful of microchips on the table.

"Thanks, Rob," Tom said. "Did you have any difficulty with those new circuits I designed?"

Tom's huge robotic assistant had begun as an experiment in artificial intelligence and gone on to be his lab associate, among many other things.

"No problemo, boss dude," Rob replied. "Orb reprogrammed your chip editor with the new specs, and voilà!"

"Rob, make a note for Orb to edit through your vocabulary file and delete some of the more colorful terms and phrases that Rick has been teaching you," Tom said with a glare at his best friend.

Rick and Dan began to laugh, and so did the girls.

"But, Tom," Rick said finally, "you wanted Rob's speech to be more conversational. I just told him to watch a couple of hours of Saturday morning TV. Orb watched, too, and he seems unaffected."

"Where *is* the little guy?" Tom asked, looking around for the spherical, basketball-size robot that had once been Rob's "brain" but was now an independent intelligent unit capable of interfacing with any electronic system. Orb was such an expert in intersystem communications that he had once done emergency duty as a geosynchronous communications satellite.

"Oh, please, no more robots!" Lisa groaned. "When Dan said we were going to a laboratory, I expected to see a chemistry set or something."

"Welcome to the wonderful world of Tom Swift," Dan said with a wave of his hand, "where you're likely to see just about anything, including the latest in electronic gadgets, solid-state physics, bioengineering, cybernetics, and interdimensional travel."

"The only place I wanted to go was the beach," Lisa said, looking around nervously.

"So was the experiment a success?" Mandy asked, glancing over Tom's shoulder at his notes.

"Well, I'm on the right track, I think. I was definitely receiving thoughts from my associate there."

Mandy's brown eyes were thoughtful. "I always believed that thought transference was just science fiction, like in the magazines I read."

"Well, that's true, as far as it goes," Tom agreed. "But then, a lot of things that *used* to be true only in science fiction are just everyday stuff now."

"Yeah, like black holes and trips to the

moon," Rick said. "Everyday stuff for Tom Swift, anyway." Rick was referring to Tom's trip to the moon in a NASA shuttle equipped with a Swift nuclear engine. The shuttle had disappeared behind the dark side of the moon, and he and everyone else had believed Tom and the rest of the crew to be dead or drifting hopelessly in space.

"Would this gizmo also work with two humans?" Mandy asked.

Tom tinkered with one of the components on his headset. "The translator hasn't been calibrated yet to read human brain waves, but that's really just a simple adjustment."

"Yeah, for you!" Rick laughed.

"Just think of it," Tom told his friends, excitement shining in his blue eyes. "When this device is working the way I've designed it to, it'll have dozens of useful applications in medicine, not to mention research into the animal kingdom." He ticked off the uses on his fingers. "Doctors will be able to communicate with patients with neurological disorders or accident victims or anyone who's lost the power of speech permanently or temporarily. In addition, we can learn a lot about the structure of thoughts in general and how the brain forms language and concepts."

"Maybe we can even figure out why *your* brain works the way it does," Mandy joked.

"Oh, no," Rick replied with a grin. "There

are some things humanity was not meant to know!"

"Tom, I think we'd better get Mickey into his carrier and back to Mary Ann," Sandra said. She and Lisa were trying to calm the cat, who had found the door to the lab and was meowing and scratching desperately.

"Okay," Tom said. "Everybody ready to go?"

Before anyone could answer, a low roaring sound came from outside. As Tom went to the window, he saw one side of his lab seem to rise up, then slam down hard, rattling glass and metal along the lab walls. There was a half second for Tom to wonder what it meant, then the once-solid floor of the lab began to pitch like an angry ocean. In a flash he realized what was happening.

"Earthquake!" Tom shouted. "Everyone get under this metal workbench!"

Rick and Dan dived beneath the bench. Mandy took a step toward Tom, then stumbled and fell to the floor. As Tom helped her scramble to safety under the bench, he saw Lisa trying to open the lab door. "Lisa! Get away from the door!" he shouted.

"I'm getting out of here!" Lisa cried, pulling at the door handle.

"No! Running outside is the wrong thing to do! Everyone get under the workbench—it's strong enough to protect us from falling equipment! Sandra, get the cat!"

9

Sandra scooped up the struggling cat and joined the others under the bench. The floor rocked and heaved like a living thing. Shelves smashed against walls and fell over, hurling glass and metal everywhere. The cat howled as heavy equipment crashed down onto the bench above them and glass exploded against the walls and floor. The noise was frightful, and Tom thought the horrible jarring and shaking would never end.

As he huddled beneath the bench with his sister and his friends, listening to their world coming apart around them, Tom couldn't fight the feeling that they were all about to die.

2

AFTER WHAT SEEMED LIKE AN ETERNITY, THE shaking stopped. Tom eased out from under the bench and stood up on unsteady legs. The lights, which had gone out during the quake, flickered back to life as the Swift Enterprises backup generators came on-line. "It's okay to come out now," he told the others.

Looking around, he saw that the lab was a shambles, with most of the lighter furniture flung about like the result of a giant's tantrum. Shelves lay on their sides, their contents scattered across the floor. Broken glass was everywhere. "Watch your feet," Tom said as he helped his sister up.

Rob, who was undamaged, helped Tom's friends emerge from the shelter of the workbench.

Rick gave a low whistle. "Look at this mess," he said. "I just want to say right now that I do *not* volunteer for the cleanup committee." He waved a hand at the crushed and damaged equipment and lab supplies that littered the floor.

"Oh, Tom!" Mandy said. "Your laboratory is ruined!"

"It's not as bad as it looks," Tom assured her as he quickly checked out some of the more valuable equipment. He managed to locate the cat carrier and held it open for Sandra so she could put the loudly meowing Mickey inside. "I don't think there's a lot of permanent damage. And the important thing is, we're all okay. Let's go outside and see what's going on."

The first thing Tom saw was his father hurrying toward the lab. A look of relief washed over the older man's face as he saw his son and daughter and their friends emerge from the lab, shaken but unhurt. "I knew the building would stand up to the quake," he said as he joined them. "All the buildings here exceed California earthquake standards, but I couldn't help worrying about you, anyway."

"We're all fine," Tom assured him. "Is anyone else injured?"

"Your mother's fine. She's checking for earthquake bulletins on TV. As for the rest of Swift Enterprises, some workers suffered bumps and bruises and a few minor lacerations. The infirmary team is already on the job. There's no structural damage to the complex, thanks to all that quake-safe designing. Now that I know you're all right, I'm on my way to the seismology lab to get a look at the readings on this baby. I understand they've already been sent by modem to CalTech to give the folks there more data to work with."

"Mind if we tag along?" Tom asked.

"Of course not," Mr. Swift said.

"You guys, I'm going to take this cat back to Mary Ann Jennings," Sandra said. "I'll catch up with you at the lab."

"We'll see you there," Mr. Swift called as he led the others away.

When they reached the seismology lab, Tom and his friends couldn't help chuckling at the hand-lettered sign on the door that read All Shook Up.

"Some joker must have put that up in the last few minutes," Mr. Swift said. He opened the door and motioned the group inside.

One of the walls of the lab was almost completely taken up with large round drums that turned continuously under slender pens mounted on delicate wires above their surface. The pens traced lines on the paper that covered the drums.

As they watched, an aftershock rumbled through the area and shook the building. The pens swung wildly as they all reached for a piece of furniture or anything stable to brace themselves against the temblor. When it was over, they all converged shakily on the seismographs.

"It looks sort of like Rick's handwriting," Dan said. "What does it mean?"

"Fortunately, we have an expert on hand to explain," said Mr. Swift. "This is Mary McKenna, a graduate student in seismology who's interning here at the lab."

"Hi!" A pretty young woman with short dark hair greeted Tom and his friends. "Anything earthshaking happen to you guys lately?"

"Nah," Rick said. "Just another dull day in California."

"So you can actually make some sense of all these chicken-scratchings?" Mandy asked Mary.

"That's what I've got everyone fooled into thinking," Mary replied in a stage whisper. "Don't give away my secret, okay?" She pointed to one of the revolving drums, where a series of almost perfectly flat lines drawn by the pens had suddenly become a violent zigzag of motion, then gradually resumed their smooth configuration.

"Here's the aftershock we just experienced," Mary told them, indicating the places where the pens had swung wildly from side to side. "Each of these pens traces a different kind of seismic wave. Some are straight-line compressive pulses, some travel up and down or side to side. Some seismic waves have an action like ocean breakers, and some even crack the earth like a bullwhip."

"And I thought geology was boring," Rick said, shaking his head.

"Not my branch of it. True, we wait a long time for things to happen, but once they do ..." She indicated all the bustle going on in the room as technicians monitored data and relayed it to remote locations. Then she waved to Sandra, who had just come into the lab.

"Hi, Mary," Sandra called. "Have I missed anything?"

"Not at all," Mary said. "I was just about to show your friends Swift Enterprises' brand-new babies." She indicated an array of several monitors, like small television screens lined up on a worktable. "They're digital broadband seismometers, prototype models. And this is their nursemaid, Hiroshi Nakamura. Hiroshi-san is a visiting scientist from Tokyo University."

A young man in a lab coat who was seated in front of the monitor array rose to greet them. "How do you do," he said with a pleasant smile. "I am very glad to meet you."

"*Konnichi wa,*" said Rick with a little bow.

"Ah," Hiroshi said, brightening. "You speak Japanese?"

"Just that one phrase," Rick admitted, turning a little red. "I heard it in a movie last week."

"Well, one phrase is a beginning," Hiroshi replied. "Would you like to see the new seismometers?"

"They look like television sets," Mandy said. "Don't they use recording drums like the ones over there?"

"These use optical media," Mary said. "Like CDs."

"It would take a stack of computer disks about three feet high to hold as much data as one little optical disk," Tom explained to the others. "You can imagine how that cuts down on storage space."

Hiroshi typed a command on the keyboard and the monitors came to life, rolling up twisting columns of numbers so fast that no one could read them. "How do you make sense of all this?" Mandy asked the young scientist.

"I do not make sense of it, but computer programs I have written do, with the help of Megatron, the supercomputer that runs Swift Enterprises. From this data we can tell not only when and where the temblor struck and how strong it was, but much more data that was once impossible to record. Each earthquake leaves a signature on these instruments as individual as a fingerprint."

"Tell us about the earthquake we just experienced," Tom urged.

Hiroshi typed in a command, and the squirming numbers began to rearrange themselves into a table of information. "The quake registered magnitude six point one on the Moment Magnitude Scale," he said. "The epicenter was three point two miles west, in the Pacific Ocean. There will, of course, be tsunami along the coast."

"I guess I know *two* Japanese words," Rick said. "Doesn't that mean tidal waves?"

"Harbor waves, to be exact," Mary replied. "Kicked up by underwater earth movement. They can do a lot of damage to ships in port, and they're very dangerous to anyone who's near the shore when they strike."

"That settles it. The beach picnic's definitely canceled," Rick said. "Do you suppose the phones work? I should call my house and let my folks know I'm all right."

"I think we'd all better do that," Mandy said.

"Our modem call went through," Mr. Swift told them, "so there shouldn't be a problem. Let's go over to the house."

Tom's friends called and reassured their families that they hadn't been hurt in the quake. Then Tom and Sandra walked the others outside and watched as they piled into Dan's and Rick's cars.

"Be careful driving," Tom cautioned. "There could be cracks in the roadbed, or even landslides."

The cars rolled down the long, winding

driveway to the road below. Tom sighed. "What a day," he remarked to his sister.

"I'll say," Sandra agreed. "Let's go inside and get the official version of what happened."

They found their mother in front of the television set. According to the news stories, she told them, the quake had caused some water-main and gas-line fractures in Los Angeles. Firefighters were working to put out fires that had started from the escaped gas. Several people had been killed by falling concrete and collapsed buildings, and there had been some damage to roadways in the western part of the country. Ships in port had been advised to put to sea before they could be damaged by the tsunami, which was expected to be of only moderate strength and would arrive at low tide.

Everyone in southern California was advised to stay away from the beaches, and several seaside communities had been evacuated by the state's Office of Emergency Services. Aftershocks were continuing at fifteen- to thirty-minute intervals, but none was as strong as the original quake.

As Tom flipped from one news show to another, one name kept cropping up: Dr. Eric Weiss, a prominent seismologist with the lab at the California Institute of Technology. Dr. Weiss had recently published some papers dealing with new theories in seismology, and he was the expert that everyone wanted to interview. Tom watched these interviews with interest and also paid attention to the statements of other seismologists, many of whom seemed to disagree with Weiss's ideas. One older seismologist in particular, Dr. Randall Moss, kept cautioning the reporters not to treat Dr. Weiss's theories as facts just yet.

Mr. Swift came in from the seismology lab and sat down next to his wife to watch the news.

"Look, Dad," Tom said. "There's the seismologist who's been on all the stations—Dr. Weiss. He's been talking about his earthquake prediction theories."

"Oh, Eric Weiss. Of course."

"You know him?" Sandra asked.

"Yes, Eric and I worked together once on an international project. He's causing quite a stir these days over at CalTech with those new theories of his, but a lot of people in the scientific community think he's going off half-cocked."

"What do *you* think, Dad?"

Mr. Swift pondered for a moment as he watched Dr. Weiss answer questions from a television reporter. "I think Eric Weiss is as careful a scientist as I've ever known. What he's saying about earthquake prediction flies in the face of everything most seismologists hold dear, but if Eric believes it, I'd say he probably has good reason."

Just then the earth rumbled, and the floor

19

shook a bit. "Goodness! I jump out of my skin every time there's another aftershock," Mrs. Swift said.

"Me, too," Sandra confessed. "I feel as if I'm going through the quake all over again."

"Believe it or not, Sandra, that's perfectly natural," Mr. Swift said. "It's part of the natural psychological aftereffects of a serious earthquake."

"How about the feeling that the walls are closing in on you?" Tom asked. "When it started getting dark a little while ago, I felt like I wanted to run outside."

"That's normal, too. An earthquake is a frightening thing. Our fears may seem irrational, but they're a result of being badly frightened by something we have no control over. It will probably take a few weeks before we're over the shock, but we'll get back to our regular routine sooner or later, I promise you."

The phone rang, and Mr. Swift reached over to pick it up. "Swift residence," he said into the receiver, then he put his hand over the mouthpiece and told the others, "It's Eric Weiss."

When he got off the telephone, Mr. Swift recounted the details of his conversation with Dr. Weiss. "He wants to visit on Monday and talk to me about setting up some special experiments. Eric's afraid that if he can't get more established seismologists like Dr. Moss to start taking his earthquake prediction theories seriously, we may miss a chance to be prepared for the next major earthquake."

"I'm still trying to recover from *this* one," remarked Mrs. Swift. "I don't think I'm going to be able to get a wink of sleep tonight."

"Me, either," Tom agreed. "If you say these feelings are normal, I believe you, Dad, but that doesn't make them any easier to deal with."

"I don't know about you," Sandra said, "but I really can't face the thought of going down the hall to my room tonight."

"Well, then," said Mr. Swift, "I have an idea that might make everyone feel better and help us get the sleep we need. Let's get the tent and our sleeping bags and camp out in the backyard!"

There was a festive atmosphere in the air in spite of the frequent rumblings of the ground as the Swifts carried sleeping bags out to the backyard. Mr. Swift pitched a camping tent big enough for the whole family while Tom lit a couple of lanterns. Mrs. Swift brought out snacks and juice, and Sandra set up a portable radio.

"Good idea, Sandra," Mr. Swift said. "We should probably keep this on in case there are any emergency bulletins during the night. I see we're all prepared. I've brought my cellular phone in case there are any emergency calls from the Swift complex late shift tonight."

"Now, that," his wife said, laughing, "is what I call roughing it!"

In spite of his feelings of uneasiness and the frequent minor tremors, Tom was soon asleep.

He woke from a dream of shrilling alarms to see his father pick up the telephone and press the On button. As Mr. Swift listened, his expression grew more and more troubled.

Tom sat up in his sleeping bag and waited to find out what was happening. "I'll be right there," Mr. Swift said in a low voice. He turned the phone off and set it down, unzipped his sleeping bag, and reached for his shoes. Mrs. Swift and Sandra were still asleep.

"Dad, what's going on?"

"That was the night security team chief at our nuclear power plant. There's been some sort of accident. Harlan's on his way from home, and I have to get down there right away. The coolant system appears to have failed. We could be headed for an atomic meltdown!"

3

TOM GRABBED HIS SNEAKERS AND HURRIED out of the tent after his father. They ran to Mr. Swift's car and raced down the hill to the Swift Enterprises nuclear power station, where lights were blazing and other vehicles were already pulling into the parking lot. Harlan Ames, Swift Enterprises' chief of security, met them at the front door, fully dressed except for his bedroom slippers, which he had forgotten to change in his haste to get to the power plant.

"The backup coolant system is up and running, and everything's under control," he told them, "but that's not the most interesting part of the story. Come and see what's waiting for us in the security office."

Harlan led the way down a series of brightly lit hallways to a small room fitted with an observation window into the security office. On the other side of the window a man wearing the blue coveralls and Swift Enterprises patch of a Swift power station employee sat in a straight-backed chair.

"The gentleman on the other side of this two-way mirror is George Perry," said Harlan. "Perry has been a low-level employee of Swift Power for about six months. Tonight, after he clocked out at the end of his shift, he went back into the plant and hid himself in a supply closet."

"I didn't think it was possible to get back through the automatic security doors," Tom said.

"It shouldn't be," Harlan agreed, "but he was carrying a hand-held device that temporarily jammed the electronic lock. A very sophisticated little piece of equipment, I might add."

"Then what happened?" Mr. Swift asked.

"It seems Perry had hidden a container of chloroform in the supply closet at some earlier time. He used that to render one security guard unconscious, then hid again and gassed the other one when he came in to investigate. Now he had the two keys he needed to get into the security locker."

"What did he need from there?" Tom asked.

"The keys to the fissionable materials storage area."

"You don't mean—" Tom started to say.

"Yep," Harlan said with a grim nod. "He took a lockbox with a vial of plutonium inside and went to make his escape. On the way past the main control panel, he seems to have fumbled the box. It fell on the panel, resetting half a dozen switches and snapping them off in the process, so they couldn't be reset. That's what caused the alarm to go off—he stopped the coolant flow to the plutonium rods."

"That fool!" Mr. Swift burst out. "He could have caused a far worse disaster than the earthquake today."

"Well, to Perry's credit, he took time out to manually activate the backup coolant system. That's how we caught him," Harlan said, shaking his head. "He's been pretty cooperative so far and agreed to answer our questions. It seems he's a member of STAND."

"What's STAND?" Tom asked.

"It's an acronym for Stop All Nuclear Devices," his father answered. "It's a group of people who are opposed to using nuclear power in any form for any reason."

"It seems to me that a guy like that wouldn't be caught dead working in a nuclear power plant—unless he had some sort of secret plan," Tom said. "Like stealing plutonium."

"That's what we think, too," said Harlan.

"Perry has been a good employee. His employment record is completely clean, and he has no police record at all—just your average citizen. But what's your average citizen doing walking around with one of these?"

Harlan reached into the top drawer of his desk and withdrew a small black device equipped with several studs and dials. Mr. Swift took it from him and looked it over, then handed it to Tom. "What do you make of this, son?" he asked him.

Tom turned the instrument over in his hand and studied it. "I've never seen anything quite like it before, but it's an elegant piece of work, all right. Is this the thing he used to jimmy the door locks?"

"Yep. And my guess is that it cost more than George Perry makes in six months. I think whoever's behind this STAND organization has some pretty heavy funding. And while that's certainly not against the law, stealing plutonium is."

"What do you know about this group, Harlan?" Mr. Swift asked.

"I have a whole file on them," Harlan said, "dating back to about a year ago when they suddenly appeared on the scene."

Harlan switched on his desktop computer and typed the command that loaded his security data base program. From a list of files onscreen he chose one called STAND and pressed the Return key. A picture appeared of a man in his middle thirties with dark hair and a mustache.

"This is the leader of the STAND organization, Edmond Audreys. It seems the FBI is very interested in Mr. Audreys. He has no criminal record, but that's because there is no record whatever of his existence before about fifteen months ago."

Harlan typed a command, and the picture shrank to one corner of the screen, while the rest was taken up with text describing various kinds of information about STAND.

"About half the organization's membership is made up of people with long and involved criminal records," Harlan said with a wry smile. "Audreys seems also to have attracted a lot of well-meaning people who really believe nuclear power should be banned—people like Mr. Perry, I imagine, but the FBI is certain he's up to something else, too, and so am I."

"I wish we knew what," Mr. Swift said, "since he seems to be involving us in his plans."

"Well, with your permission," said Harlan, "I'd like to take some steps to find out. A private investigation."

"You're a fine detective, Harlan," Mr. Swift said, "but you're too valuable around here for me to spare you, especially after this."

"I don't mean me, personally," Harlan said. "I had someone else in mind." He turned back to his computer and brought up his personnel files. Choosing one, he displayed a photograph of a woman in her late twenties with dark hair and olive skin.

"This is Jessie Gonzalez," Harlan said. "She's been working for Swift Enterprises for only a few months, but she has extensive experience in undercover work. She's barely five feet tall and weighs ninety pounds soaking wet, so bad guys don't take her seriously, but she has a second-degree black belt in aikido that proves them wrong when necessary. I think she's just the one for the job. If she's willing, I'd like to ask her to infiltrate STAND and get information back to us. We could forward anything we find out to the state and federal authorities, of course."

"Suppose Perry gets out on bail and IDs her," Mr. Swift said.

"He's never laid eyes on her," said Harlan. "She's been working the main complex, and he has no clearance there. So what do you think?"

"I think it's an excellent idea, and I'll leave the details to you."

"If she decides to take the job," Tom said, "send her by my lab. I'll have Rob manufacture some of the gizmos I designed recently for miniaturized surveillance equipment."

"And now," said Mr. Swift, turning back to the observation window that looked into the office where George Perry was being held, "how about Mr. Perry there?"

"The police are on the way," Harlan said, "but I thought you might like to talk to him first."

"Yes, I'd like to hear what he has to say for himself," said Mr. Swift. "Let's go in." He opened the door to the office, and Tom and Harlan followed him in.

Perry sat sullenly in the chair, staring at the wall. "You understand, Mr. Perry," Mr. Swift told him after he had introduced himself, "that you don't have to answer any of our questions. When the police get here, they'll explain your rights under the law."

"I already told my story to Mr. Ames," Perry said. "I don't have anything to hide. I know I'm going to jail, and I don't care."

"I guess what I'd really like to know," said Mr. Swift, taking a chair opposite Perry's, "is why you did it? Why would you steal plutonium, knowing how dangerous it is?"

"That's the whole point!" Perry cried. "I'm a member of STAND! I was stealing the plutonium to call attention to the dangers of nuclear power!

"We're trying to get the state to close down every nuclear power facility in California," Perry continued with a defiant glare. "Mr. Audreys figured that if people knew how easy it was to steal plutonium from nuclear plants, they'd pressure the governor into closing them."

"I can guarantee you it won't be so easy to get any plutonium out of Swift Power from now on," Harlan said grimly. "We're totally upgrading our security procedures, evidently something we should have done before tonight."

"Mr. Perry, are you aware that Edmond Audreys has been under investigation by the FBI for various criminal activities?" Mr. Swift asked him.

"That's right!" Perry sneered. "That's because the government is trying to undermine our efforts to ban nuclear power!"

"Are you aware that a lot of members of STAND have criminal pasts?" Harlan asked. "And your Mr. Audreys doesn't seem to have any past at all."

"Maybe Mr. Perry can give us some useful information about Audreys," Tom suggested.

"I said I'd cooperate," said Perry, "but I won't betray any of my fellow STAND members. I'll tell you this, though. Edmond Audreys is only acting in the best interests of all humanity. And he'll stop at nothing to halt the spread of nuclear power."

"That's a pretty strong statement, Mr. Perry," said Harlan. "Do you think he'd actually endanger lives to get his message across?"

"Of course not!" Perry exclaimed. "I didn't

mean anything like that. Edmond Audreys is a great humanitarian."

Tom and Harlan exchanged glances. "I'm not sure I agree," Tom said. "What kind of humanitarian asks people to steal plutonium? If Audreys wanted to make a point, I'm sure he could find a less dangerous way to do it."

George Perry looked angrily at Tom for a moment, then lowered his gaze.

"Thank you, Mr. Perry," Mr. Swift said. "The police should be here shortly to take you into custody. I'll be sure to tell them that you've been cooperative with us, and also that you averted a disaster when you could have got away. That should be helpful at your trial."

"Thanks, Mr. Swift. I appreciate everything you're doing for me, it's just that this was something I had to do. It was an act of conscience. I hope you understand."

"I'm not sure I do," Mr. Swift said, shaking his head. "I think an act of conscience needs to be a moral act as well, and one that doesn't needlessly endanger others. At any rate, this is over now."

A man in a security uniform walked in and handed Harlan a folded slip of paper. Harlan read it with a frown, then led the Swifts out of the security office and into a nearby waiting room, where someone had put on a pot of coffee. He poured himself a cup, then turned to Tom and his father.

"I'm not sure this *is* all over."

"What do you mean?" Mr. Swift asked.

"In the past three weeks two other nuclear facilities in the southern California area have come up short in their fissionable materials inventory—missing plutonium, weapons-grade."

"Do you think these STAND people are responsible?" Tom asked, exchanging a glance with his father.

"I think after tonight the police will be looking into that connection," Harlan said. "And of course we'll pursue our own investigation with Jessie."

"I'd like to meet her," said Mr. Swift. "Why don't you bring her by my office first thing tomorrow? Then we can get Tom to equip her and get started with your plan to infiltrate STAND."

"Good, because I don't think there's a minute to lose," said Harlan. He held up the slip of paper he'd been given in the holding room. "I've made some calls to verify the amounts of fissionable material missing from the other plants. Assuming STAND is responsible for those thefts, too—and I don't think we can afford to assume they're not," he said, "then, even if you don't count what George Perry tried to take out of here tonight, enough weapons-grade plutonium is missing from plants within a hundred and twenty-five-mile radius of Swift Enterprises for anyone with the proper know-how to construct a sizable atomic bomb."

4

WHEN TOM'S ALARM RANG ON MONDAY morning, he didn't feel all that ready to start the day. He'd had trouble sleeping, alternately worrying about sudden seismic aftershocks and the missing plutonium. But he had a lot of work ahead of him before noon, and he'd promised Harlan some Swift-style gadgets. He dragged himself out of bed and into the shower. "Let's roll, Swift," he said to his bleary-eyed reflection in the mirror. "Time to play boy inventor."

Sandra was at the breakfast table, looking nearly as bad as Tom felt. "You don't look as if you slept any better than I did," Tom said, pouring them both glasses of orange juice.

"I think I was awake all night," Sandra

said. "Either being frightened by an aftershock or waiting for one to frighten me."

"It's summer," Tom told her. "Go back to bed."

"I wouldn't sleep, anyway. Need any help in the lab this morning?"

"Well, if you're going to be there, we could do some test runs on the psychotronic translator, but what I really need is some of your jewelry."

Sandra raised an eyebrow. "I don't think it'd look that great on you," she said, buttering a waffle.

Tom rolled his eyes. "Not for me. I need it for some miniature snooping equipment for Jessie Gonzalez. Just a couple of everyday things, not fancy, that you don't wear anymore."

"Yeah, I think I can come up with something. I'll bring some stuff to you at the lab later, and you can choose what you want, okay?"

When Tom arrived at his lab, Rob and Orb were already at work testing some of Tom's preliminary designs. Orb had hooked himself into Tom's computer-assisted design program and was feeding Rob precise measurements from the three-dimensional models Tom had built inside the CAD. Rob was inventorying materials and readying a clean room for manufacturing new chips.

"We'll have these surveillance components ready to test in an hour or so, Tom," Rob called from his workbench. "How's that new PT design coming?"

"Still mostly in my head, Rob, but when Orb's through with my CAD, I'll knock out a few plans for you to try."

"I have downloaded everything I require, Tom," said Orb. "You can access your files now."

"Thanks, Orb, you're a pal. And thanks for adjusting Rob's vocabulary file."

"I do endeavor to be helpful, Tom," Orb replied.

Sandra showed up a few minutes later with some of her old jewelry. Tom chose a plain black watch and a silver pendant and turned them over to Rob. "Now let's test out my latest recalibrations on the PT," Tom said.

Sandra took a tablet and pencil and went to sit in a glass booth Rob had constructed for the PT tests. The booth was soundproof and had a microphone link to the rest of the lab.

"Is this thing working?" she called over Tom's speaker system as she picked up her PT headset.

"I read you loud and clear, sis," Tom responded. He glanced up at his door monitor. "Here comes Dad—maybe he wants to watch the test."

His voiceprint confirmed, Mr. Swift strode

into the lab, accompanied by someone whom Tom recognized.

"Tom, this is Dr. Eric Weiss," Mr. Swift said, introducing his guest. "I'm sure you remember him from television."

"I'm pleased to meet you, Dr. Weiss." Tom removed his psychotronic translator headset and shook the older man's hand.

Dr. Weiss was a dark-haired man who appeared to be in his thirties, with intelligent brown eyes framed behind a pair of wire-rimmed glasses. "I'm glad to finally get the chance to meet you, too, Tom. I've heard a lot about you from your father, but I'm afraid I've written most of it off as paternal pride. Are you really everything he tells me you are?"

"Well, Dad brags a lot," Tom said, "but I do like to tinker with new technology."

"Tom's being modest, as usual," Mr. Swift said with a laugh. "Right now he and my daughter, Sandra—that's her on the other side of that glass partition—are conducting experiments with a very promising new invention of Tom's that might someday revolutionize communications. Right now it's showing surprisingly good results reading thoughts remotely."

"Mind reading!" Dr. Weiss snorted. "I thought Swift Enterprises used its resources only to explore genuine scientific developments. Mind reading is nothing but pseudoscience."

"That may have been true before now, Dr. Weiss," Tom broke in, "but the psychotronic translator really works. Look here. Sandra is going to draw some geometric shapes in random order on a tablet she's holding behind that partition. Before she draws each shape, she's going to think about it for a few seconds. I'll be attempting to draw each shape before she does."

He put on his headset and picked up a microphone. "Ready, Sandra?"

"Ready." Sandra's voice came into Tom's side of the lab over a loudspeaker.

"Okay, start thinking about the first shape."

Sandra closed her eyes and concentrated. Tom picked up a pencil and tablet and began to draw a square, followed by a circle, a triangle, another square, a trapezoid, and a five-pointed star.

"Okay, that's enough for a test run," Tom told Sandra. "Bring your tablet in here and let's compare." He turned to Dr. Weiss. "If the PT is working properly, my batch of drawings and Sandra's should be identical and in the same order on the page."

"That headset looks a lot different from the one you were working on before the earthquake," Mr. Swift commented to Tom.

"I've streamlined it and made some internal improvements, too. The electronics are more refined now—the carrier wave is a stream of ultraviolet light that projects from the sender's set to the receiver. The thought transmissions are carried as pulses along the photon stream."

"You did all that in the past two days?" Mr. Swift's eyebrows shot up. "I guess I shouldn't be surprised, but you certainly have been busy this morning."

"Well, I had a breakthrough, and one thing just sort of led to another. I had a lot of help from Rob with the actual construction of the components."

"Who's Rob?" Dr. Weiss asked. "Another Swift son?"

"Not exactly," Mr. Swift said, chuckling. "Here he comes now."

The gleaming humanoid robot entered from a back room of the lab, carrying a small tray with an array of tiny processor chips. "How do you like this batch, Tom?" he asked. "Cooked 'em up special myself."

"They look great, Rob. We'll test them out later, but first I'd like you to meet Dr. Eric Weiss of the California Institute of Technology."

Dr. Weiss stared in surprise as Rob extended a shiny hand. "Pleased to meet you, Dr. Weiss," the robot offered. "Any friend of Tom's is a friend of mine."

Dr. Weiss held out a hand, and Rob shook it. "Well, I have a lot to do back in the clean room," Rob said. "I'm going to start work on that surveillance gear Tom designed for Jessie Gonzalez. Nice to meet you, Dr. Weiss."

Dr. Weiss continued to stare as Rob closed the door to his workshop behind him. Finally he shook his head as though to clear it. "I don't know how you pulled that one off, but I'm impressed," he said to Tom.

"Oh, Rob's for real, too," Mr. Swift assured him. "He's part of an ongoing artificial intelligence project of Tom's. Here comes Sandra with her tablet—let's take a look, shall we?"

Sandra handed her tablet to Tom. After introducing her to Dr. Weiss, Mr. Swift looked over the two pieces of paper. "It's just as you thought, Tom," he said, comparing the two sets of drawings. "You've drawn the same shapes in the same order as Sandra. It looks like the PT is working just fine."

"After a few more tests, I'd like to see if I can refine the transmission scheme even further," Tom said, "but don't expect to see any more major improvements for a day or two."

"You see, Eric," Mr. Swift said to Dr. Weiss, "Tom's continuing research into new technologies has proved helpful to Swift Enterprises on many occasions."

Dr. Weiss took a step back, distrust clouding his dark eyes. "This is some kind of joke, isn't it? And you're all in on it. Well, it may be amusing to play 'fool the scientist,' but I don't have time for this kind of foolishness."

Mr. Swift rushed to reassure his colleague. "You don't understand, Eric. Tom isn't an amateur magician, he's a scientist in the best sense of the word, and he would never waste his own or anyone else's time with tricks. Why don't you take a turn at the sender's set yourself and see if Tom can pick up something from you?"

Dr. Weiss looked at Tom, then back at Mr. Swift. "All right, if you insist, I'll try it." Sandra let him into the booth behind the soundproof glass and showed him how to put on the headset.

"Frame your thought clearly," Tom instructed him. "Let me know when you're ready to send."

"Ready," Dr. Weiss said immediately.

Tom concentrated, but nothing seemed to be coming through. After a moment Dr. Weiss snatched the PT impatiently from his head. "I knew it wouldn't work," he said over the loudspeaker. "Now can we get out of here? I have important work to do, and time is short."

"The PT might work better if you visualize something, Dr. Weiss," Tom suggested. "The translator isn't calibrated finely enough yet to interpret abstract ideas. Try picturing one thing clearly in your mind, and I'll see if I can receive it. If this trial is no good, I guess I'll go back to the drawing board."

"All right, but this is my last shot," Dr.

Weiss said, putting the headset back on. He closed his eyes.

On the other side of the glass Tom picked up his pencil and began to draw. He tried not to think about what he was drawing, because the image wasn't recognizable—just a lot of lines going in different directions and some circles and arrows. After a few minutes Tom said, "This is what I received. Take a look and tell me if I got close."

Dr. Weiss came out of the booth and took the paper in his hand. "Yes, that's it. That's what I was thinking of."

"But what is it?" Sandra asked, turning the paper this way and that to try to make sense of the lines.

Dr. Weiss took another piece of paper out of his pocket and showed them a piece of a California map with inked lines drawn on top of the southern California region. The lines and other figures were identical in spacing and direction to the ones Tom had drawn.

"What does this mean, Eric?" Mr. Swift asked.

"It's a diagram of the major fault zones that run underneath southern California. The arrows indicate likely shear zones along the fault lines. The circles are spheres of devastation we can expect from an earthquake of more than magnitude eight. That would be the monster quake that's been dreaded for decades—and the one I'm predicting will hit southern California in less than two weeks."

"Wait a second," Tom said as he looked at the map. "According to this, *we're* right in the middle of the danger zone. If your calculations are correct, in two weeks Swift Enterprises will be just one gigantic gaping hole in the earth!"

5

HOW MUCH DO YOU KNOW ABOUT EARTH-quakes?" Dr. Weiss asked the Swifts after they were gathered in a conference room at the Swift Enterprises seismology lab. Several large pull-down maps adorned one wall, showing the fault lines under California, the historic record of California quakes, and the places along the faults most likely to suffer severe earthquakes in the near future.

"Probably more than the average person," said Mr. Swift. "I know that we're living in an extremely active area for quakes. Until now I've tended to leave the details to the experts, like the technicians and graduate students here at the lab," Mr. Swift continued. "I'm afraid I haven't made seismology a specialty."

"Same goes for me," Tom said. "I could probably take a seismometer apart and put it back together again, but I've never really studied the forces that make it go."

"Well, in a very real sense the earth is a machine," Dr. Weiss mused. "It's made up of moving parts, and each interacts with the others in predictable ways, but it's the results of those interactions that aren't quite so predictable."

"Why don't you fill us in, Eric?" Mr. Swift said. "And tell us about those new earthquake prediction theories of yours that have your colleagues so up in arms."

"All right," Dr. Weiss said as he walked over to one of the wall maps, which showed the earth separated into large sections. "The outer layer of the earth's crust—the lithosphere—is broken up into a number of tectonic plates, as you see on this map. The plates are in constant motion, sometimes shifting as much as ten centimeters a year."

"Not exactly a breakneck ride," Tom commented.

"No, but it *is* a bumpy one," said Dr. Weiss. "The plates don't just make way for one another—they collide at certain places. And at several key spots beneath the oceans, the plates move *away* from one another. This allows magma rising from the earth's core to form new ocean floor."

He pointed at some locations under the

major oceans. "But at Convergent Zones such as this place off the Pacific Coast of California, two plates collide head-on. Where one dives beneath the other, it's called a Subduction Zone. It was this kind of movement off the southern California coast that caused the most recent quake.

"But there's a third type of plate movement," Dr. Weiss continued. "It's the one this whole state lives in fear of." He pointed at a fault map, where a large single fracture split the Pacific Coast in a nearly straight line from Cape Mendocino in the north all the way down to Los Angeles.

"Isn't that the San Andreas Fault?" Sandra asked.

"Yes, it is. The fault is over eight hundred miles long, and it's an example of the third type of plate border—the Shear Zone."

"That must be the type where two plates are moving past each other in opposite directions and get blocked," Tom offered.

"Exactly," said Dr. Weiss. "The San Andreas is the border between the Pacific and North American plates. The Pacific plate, here on the left, is moving northward at about five centimeters a year."

"Does that mean that Los Angeles is heading for Alaska?" asked Tom.

"Yes, but it won't arrive for about sixty million years, and the movement wouldn't be much of a problem except that the slip of the two plates isn't constant. The Pacific plate is actually moving faster in the central part of the fault, and slower at the northern and southern ends. Friction, or clamping stress, as we refer to it, has kept this portion of the faultline from moving significantly since 1857. It hasn't moved in any major way in about three hundred years."

"So that means when it does move," Sandra said, "it's probably going to move a lot."

"And expend a fantastic amount of energy," Tom added.

"And that will be the 'big one,' as we non-seismologists call it," Mr. Swift said thoughtfully.

"Seismologists call it that, too," said Dr. Weiss, "and we're always waiting for it. The southern San Andreas is the hottest potential earthquake zone in North America, and all eyes in the seismological community are watching it—nervously. Twenty million people live along the San Andreas Fault. A quake in the range of magnitude seven—that is to say, a pretty severe quake—would cause thousands of deaths and hundreds of millions of dollars in lost property. But the quake I believe is coming will be around magnitude eight, or ten times as powerful as a magnitude seven."

"Magnitude eight," said Mr. Swift, shaking his head. "Even with our earthquake-resistant construction, I don't think the Swift Enterprises complex, including the nuclear power plant, could possibly survive such a quake without considerable damage. And if the power plant were in operation at the time . . ."

"Dr. Weiss, you said the quake *you* believe is coming," Tom said. "Don't other experts agree?"

"Yes and no." Dr. Weiss shrugged. "They all agree it's coming, but it's my time line, among other things, that has the more conservative seismologists thinking I've slipped a gear."

Dr. Weiss put his briefcase up on the conference table and opened it. He took out a batch of printouts and spread them on the tabletop.

Tom picked up one and looked at it. The page was filled with groups of numbers that seemed meaningless.

"The numbers you see represent data recorded and analyzed by SAM."

"A colleague of yours?" asked Mr. Swift.

"In a manner of speaking." Dr. Weiss laughed. "SAM stands for Seismic Anomaly Modeler. It's a computer program I wrote to collect large amounts of data to help predict the location and severity of future quakes. As you probably know, predicting when and where a quake will strike, and how severe that quake will be, has been anything but an exact science, but that was before SAM."

"What does SAM do, exactly, to predict earthquakes?" Sandra asked.

"One thing it does is analyze the data I give it according to theories I've developed about patterns of fault movement and the relationships between one fault and another. Algorithms representing those theories are part of the program itself."

"So SAM thinks a lot like you," Tom ventured.

"Well, it's not intelligent by any stretch of the imagination, but it's what they call an expert system, and I guess you could say I'm the expert it takes after."

Dr. Weiss pulled another piece of paper from the briefcase. "SAM also processes the data into maps of the fault system deep underground, where earthquakes begin. These maps are considerably more accurate and more detailed than any that can be provided by the technology in use at CalTech. Knowing where these faults are gives us the ability to add artificial pressure. You see, if a fault could be made to move a little bit at a time instead of all at once, the violent surface results of the movement wouldn't occur."

"But how could you make the fault move only a little bit?" Sandra asked.

"I think I know," Tom said. "You could lubricate it, like stuck parts in a machine. Then the plates could slip a little at a time."

"That's right," Dr. Weiss said, nodding in approval. "And if you could also trigger sympathetic vibrations in underground chambers deep inside the earth, gasses would be released into the fault, making the slippage even easier."

"Is that possible, Dr. Weiss?" Tom asked.

"I believe it is. If SAM can have access to the advanced equipment you're testing here, I can get a whole new picture of the condition of the fault zone throughout the lithosphere. That will tell me the most beneficial place to ease the fault stress. I believe I have an almost perfectly accurate tool for earthquake forecasting, and that I'll be able to prove it with the help of Swift Enterprises. But time is running out."

Dr. Weiss pulled another map out of his briefcase and laid it on the conference table for the others to see. "This is a map SAM made which includes data from Saturday's quake," he said.

Tom looked at the map. This one was a little easier to understand, with a map of the Pacific Coast broken up into colored zones.

Dr. Weiss continued. "Areas which are fairly safe from major plate movement in the next thirty years or so are colored green. There are also some orange areas as you can see. Those mean a likelihood of damaging quakes in the future, but not in the next thirty to forty years."

"What do the red zones mean?" Tom asked, although he already had a good idea.

Dr. Weiss indicated a red zone that covered

a large portion of southern California, including Los Angeles, Central Hills, and the sites of all three nuclear plants Harlan had mentioned. "The red zones indicate immediate danger of a killer earthquake of magnitude eight or higher," he said. "And we're sitting right in the middle of the biggest one."

6

MR. SWIFT LOOKED UP FROM THE MAP. "ERIC, I'm proposing that Swift Enterprises put all available resources into your project, starting immediately."

"Then you believe my theories are accurate?"

"I don't think we can afford not to. Just tell us what you need, and we'll get it for you."

"I'll need to use your seismology lab and all its equipment, for a start," said Dr. Weiss. "Those new broadband digital seismometers of yours will help give me better and more complete data to put into SAM."

"I just want you to know," Tom offered, "that I'm available to give you any help you need. I'm prepared to put all my other projects on hold indefinitely."

Dr. Weiss looked puzzled. "But how could you help?" he asked.

"I told you, Eric," Mr. Swift said, putting an arm around Tom's shoulders, "my son is a very able scientist and a crackerjack engineer. I think his assistance would be extremely beneficial to your project, but of course the final decision is up to you."

Dr. Weiss shook his head. "I'm sorry, but I don't think Tom's help will be needed. I'm certain the resources here at the lab will be more use to me than a teenage boy."

Sandra and Tom exchanged glances, and Tom could see that Sandra was as puzzled as he was about Dr. Weiss's attitude toward him.

"Well, then, Tom," Mr. Swift said, "why don't you and Sandra go back to work on the psychotronic translator project? I'll check in so you can update me on your progress."

"Okay, Dad," Tom said. He didn't want Dr. Weiss to see his disappointment in not being included in an exciting research and field project, but he knew his father understood.

Mr. Swift walked with Tom and Sandra to the conference room door. "I'll keep you up-to-date on the SAM project, too," he promised. "Eric's just feeling a bit territorial about his pet venture right now, but he'll come around, don't you worry."

"I hope so, Dad. Meanwhile, I'll keep busy on the PT. You're going to see some great improvements over the next couple of days," Tom promised.

"I have no doubt of that," said Mr. Swift, smiling at his son.

Tom looked at his watch as he and his sister crossed the grounds from the seismology lab to his own laboratory. "Looks like I still have an hour to get together some equipment for Jessie Gonzalez's investigation into STAND," he told Sandra.

"Tom, aren't you upset about Dr. Weiss shutting you out of his earthquake project?"

"Yeah, I have to admit I am, but I don't want to waste time feeling hurt about it when I can be getting important things of my own done."

"I understand that, but just the same, none of Swift Enterprises' resident researchers has ever treated you like a troublesome child. Dr. Weiss's attitude just makes me so angry!"

"Well, the resident scientists and technicians know me a lot better than Dr. Weiss does. Don't forget, they were all a little surprised when they first met me, too." These days Tom's input was not only accepted but frequently asked for by the researchers. "If I can figure out some way to make myself indispensable to the earthquake project, I think Dr. Weiss will come around, too."

"I hope you're right, Tom. Do you want to run another test on the PT this afternoon?"

"No, I have to get ready for Harlan's undercover agent. Why don't you come by tomorrow, and we'll give it another run-through."

"Sure thing. See you later!" Sandra turned off the path and headed toward the Swift family residence. Tom continued on to the lab.

"Hey, Rob!" Tom called into the lab. "How are you coming on those little toys for Jessie Gonzales?" Tom had set Rob the task of assembling some miniature electronic devices that Jessie might find helpful in her undercover work.

"See for yourself," Rob said. "I think I've outdone myself."

Just then the door sounded a tone that announced a visitor. Tom glanced up at the monitor and saw Jessie waiting to be let in. "Here comes our customer. You can show her yourself." He pushed a button on a console, and the door hissed open.

The slight but well-muscled young woman walked in and shook hands with Tom. Then she stood, looking around in admiration. "This is some setup you've got here, Tom. I've heard a lot about it, but the descriptions just don't do it justice."

"Well, I hope this won't be your last visit. I've designed a few things for the security teams, and I'm always open to new ideas."

"That's right—you designed those infrared glasses I've used on night patrols."

"Yep. I hope they come in handy."

"Do they ever! So what do you have to make my life easier today?"

"Let's go see Rob. He has the items I designed up and running."

"Hello, Rob," Jessie said as they came around one of the modular lab walls to his worktable. "Do you remember me? We met a few months ago over by the new explosives lab."

"I never forget a voiceprint, Ms. Gonzalez," Rob said. "Tom and I have made a few toys for you. Want to see?"

"Of course. Dazzle me, Rob."

"No problem," the robot replied. "First, feast your eyes on this miniaturized camera setup."

He handed her what looked like a silver pendant on a chain. The pendant was in the shape of a sunburst with a smooth silver center and radiating spikes like the rays of a stylized sun.

"This is a piece of jewelry!" Jessie exclaimed.

"Yes, and it's also what Rob says it is," said Tom. "The lens is in the center behind a tiny one-way mirror. These two pieces"—he pressed on the spikes on either side of the center— "control the shutter. I just took Rob's picture."

"You mean there's film inside this thing?" Jessie said, her eyes wide in astonishment. "Where does it fit?"

"Not film," Rob corrected. "Magnetic oxide

particles on an ultrathin carrier of Swift my-lexine. The pictures are digitally recorded."

"Like on a computer disk?" Jessie asked.

"Exactly," Tom said. "Now look on the back." He turned the pendant over and re-moved the back cover. When he tipped it, a tiny phone connector attached to the pendant by ultrathin multicolored wires fell out. "When you've taken a dozen pictures, which is all the disk has room for, you can download the information digitally using any ordinary phone. I'll give you a number to call. The number will reach a computer in the security control center that's set up to receive your transmissions."

"You mean, so if I don't get back, the evi-dence will?" Jessie gave Tom a knowing look.

"Don't even think that," Tom told her. "We're taking every precaution to make this job as safe as possible. This"—he picked up a plain-looking black wristwatch—"radios your location to Swift Enterprises security con-stantly. It also has a supersensitive micro-phone and digital recording chip inside, so you can record conversations. If you get in trouble, you press this"—he indicated a tiny switch atop the watch stem—"and a distress signal is relayed back to us along with your location. Then we send someone to get you out."

"So this is the panic button," Jessie said

thoughtfully, looking at the switch. "I hope I never have to use it."

"You probably won't. Harlan has gone to a lot of trouble to create a cover identity that will withstand just about any test Edmond Audreys or his people can put it through. He has a lot of confidence in you—he wouldn't have picked you for the job if he didn't think you were up to it."

"You're right, Tom," Jessie said with a confident smile. She buckled the watch onto her wrist. "It's probably going to be a piece of cake. I really don't know how to thank you for the loan of these gizmos."

"Well," Tom said thoughtfully, "there is one little thing you could do for me. If you see any item known to have belonged to Edmond Audreys—an item of clothing, anything at all— send it here to my lab as soon as possible."

"I don't understand," Jessie said, looking confused.

"I need it for a sort of experiment I want to do. If the experiment works, I'll tell you all about it. If it flops, I've spared myself the embarrassment."

"You're the genius," Jessie said, smiling. "Now show me again how to use everything."

The following morning Sandra showed up at Tom's lab for another test run of the psychotronic translator. "Are you planning to take Mandy to Linda Brickowski's party Friday night?" she asked him as she slipped on her PT headset. "I'm going with Rick."

"I don't think so," Tom replied. "There's just so much going on here. I'd feel better if I stayed and went over the reports on the earthquake project. Dr. Weiss has SAM up and running with our data from the quake, and the analyses are starting to come in."

"Honestly, Tom, do you understand any of that gibberish that SAM spits out?"

"I admit it's tough going, but I think I'm beginning to have an idea what it all means," Tom told his sister. "And I'm still working on making myself helpful to Dr. Weiss."

"Oh, give up on that guy and come to the party," urged Sandra. "Mandy's going to be awfully disappointed when she finds out you're not going."

"Probably, but I hope she'll understand my reasons. Tell you what—how would you like to take the PT to the party? I've got a new prototype that's so small, no one will know you're wearing it."

"Really? You mean it?"

"Really. Come here and try it on."

Sandra removed the bulky headset she was wearing and came around the glass wall to take the one Tom was offering her. The new one was less than half the size of the previous model. It was now a horseshoe-shaped narrow silver band attached to what looked like a miniature flashlight about an inch long.

Tom helped her place it on her head. The flashlight portion was hidden by her hair, and the silver band looked like an ordinary headband. "Where's the other set?" asked Sandra.

"This is the whole banana," said Tom. "The infrared waves are sent out, bounce off the subject's retina, then return to the receiver carrying the thought patterns."

"This is really fantastic!" Sandra said. "Who'd believe I was wearing an invention that lets me read minds?"

"Nobody. That's the beauty of it. You can amaze and confound your friends with demonstrations of mysterious telepathy." Tom grinned. "Oh, and while you're at it, take some mental notes and let me know how it performs."

"I should have known you'd turn fun into an experiment," Sandra chided.

"Experiments *are* fun. Don't tell me you're not going to enjoy seeing the looks on all those people's faces. Meanwhile, I'll be working on the next generation of PT technology. Take a look at this."

Tom showed Sandra an even smaller PT consisting of a tiny button smaller than a dime. He pressed it onto the side of his head near his ear, where it lay flat. "This one emits an electron beam instead of UV light. It should permit even finer focusing. Of course it doesn't work yet"—he sighed as he removed the button—"but I'm sure it will soon. I just need to make a few major adjustments."

"Well, thanks for the loan of the PT, Tom. I'll stick around and run it through some tests with you if you want, but I'm going to leave it up to you to call Mandy and tell her you won't be at the party."

There was a loud beep from Tom's video monitor, and Mr. Swift came onscreen. "Tom! I'm switching you over to Channel Four— there's a news bulletin coming in!" The screen went blank, and then the face of a news reporter appeared. Behind her was a graphic of a nuclear power plant with a mushroom cloud rising in the background.

"We have received a recorded message from Edmond Audreys, head of the antinuclear group STAND, or Stop All Nuclear Devices. We now go to the message from Mr. Audreys."

The reporter disappeared, and in her place was a dark-haired man with piercing blue eyes. He faced an unseen camera, a slight smile curling on his lips.

"To the citizens of California—greetings from STAND. For months we have been warning you of the dangers of nuclear power. We have used every peaceful means at our disposal to convince the government to close existing nuclear power facilities. Our efforts have been unsuccessful.

"We have recently obtained from operating

nuclear plants enough weapons-grade pluto-nium to build a low-yield nuclear device."

"Just as we suspected," Tom said.

"If the state of California does not shut down *all* existing nuclear plants by midnight on Saturday," Audreys went on, "we will det-onate this device underground in the vicinity of one of three southern California facilities that are currently operating at full capacity."

"How could anyone be so low!" Sandra exclaimed.

"I'm beginning to think nothing's too low for Edmond Audreys," Tom replied.

Audreys leaned in closer to the camera. "The resulting explosion will have the effect of breaking up the bedrock under the plants, making them far too hazardous to operate and forcing the state to close them permanently.

"This is *not* an empty threat. The state must either close the plants now or evacuate millions of residents and watch what happens when the ground beneath the nuclear power plants begins to quake!"

7

THEY WANT TO EXPLODE A NUCLEAR DEVICE IN this area? But that could trigger the biggest quake this state has ever experienced!" Dr. Weiss exclaimed, pacing up and down the length of the conference room.

"I never thought it would come to this," admitted Harlan. "We're lucky Jessie Gonzalez made contact with STAND today. We can use her help now more than ever."

"Has SAM come up with any new insights into the last quake?" Tom asked Dr. Weiss.

"I'm waiting on the latest analysis right now," said Dr. Weiss. "SAM is sending me updates by modem twice a day."

"Meanwhile," Mr. Swift said, "we're proceeding with plans to create a tight-beam ultrasonic cannon that will use high-frequency sound to liquefy some of the solid rock deep inside the fault. That should ease some of the shear stress. We have permission from Cal-Tech to place the cannon in the holes they've already dug to monitor deep fault activity—that will save us days of extra work digging our own holes."

"And we're also going to need the state's permission to conduct the experiment," Dr. Weiss said, "but I expect we'll have it quite soon. Meanwhile, we're going to be making a trip out to CalTech's fault-line monitors to set up some tracking devices of our own. The only thing we could really use now is an uplink to the GPS."

"What's that?" Tom asked. Maybe this was something he'd be able to do for the project at last.

"The Global Positioning System," Dr. Weiss explained. "It's a satellite link to the fault-line monitors. It detects the slightest shift in relative position between one monitor and another and notifies ground stations."

"If we had a way to send and receive that kind of information instantaneously," Mr. Swift said with a meaningful look at Tom, "it could be very helpful to us."

"Let me put Orb to work on it," said Tom. "He might be able to come up with a quick solution."

"I don't know," said Dr. Weiss. "I'm not

really comfortable with the idea of having a high school student and his pet robot doing work on such a critical project."

"We won't argue Tom's training now, Eric," said Mr. Swift, "but you need something right away, and all our other resources are strained to the limit. You might want to consider accepting Tom's help."

"Well, all right then, but only on the uplink problem," Dr. Weiss said reluctantly.

"You won't regret it, Dr. Weiss," Tom promised.

An hour later Tom was back in his lab. "You *can* do it, can't you, Orb?" Tom asked the little robot.

"I do not foresee a problem," Orb answered, "but then foresight is not a part of my programming, unlike Dr. Weiss's SAM."

"Orb! I don't believe it—you're jealous!"

"Not at all," replied the spherical robot in its perpetually calm voice. "I was simply pointing out a difference between us. In many other areas I am certain I am superior to SAM, since it is a highly specialized system, while I am a generalist."

"Well, I wouldn't trade you for a hundred SAMs, Orb. I want you to get to work on the uplink now. Call me as soon as you have something."

"Of course, Tom," said Orb, floating out of

the lab on an invisible stream of magnetic levitation. "I'm working on it already."

During the afternoon Rick, Dan, and Mandy stopped by the lab, and Tom filled them in on the happenings of the past few days. "So now you can see why I've been too busy to do anything else," he told them.

"Even too busy to make a phone call, evidently," Mandy remarked.

Tom gave Mandy a shamefaced look. "I've been meaning to call, really. It's just that there are so many things going on at once, and they're so important. Not that I'm saying you're not important, but—"

"Oh, boy, is Tom in trouble now," Dan observed, shaking his head.

"Maybe we should take cover before the explosion," said Rick.

"Oh, I'm not mad," Mandy said, keeping her tone light. "But I do admit to being disappointed. And Sandra tells me you're not even planning to go to Linda Brickowski's party. I think I should have heard that from you."

"You're right," Tom admitted. "I promise not to get so distracted again that I can't stay in touch. So to help make up for my rudeness, how would you guys like to help me field-test the psychotronic translator? I need some figures on the maximum distance this thing will transmit and receive."

"Sounds like fun," Mandy said. "Do we get

to go up on stage with you when you receive your Nobel prize?"

"Absolutely. Dan, you and I will take one headset, and Mandy and Rick will take the other one. We'll go outside and measure off a distance of twenty-five feet for starters, then work our way up."

"Say, Tom," Dan said, picking up a headset, "is there any reason we can't do all this scientific inquiry at the beach?"

"Yeah," Rick said. "Don't you need to calibrate for salinity or some such thing?"

Tom laughed. "You've got me, guys. The beach is as good a place as any for this test, but I absolutely have to be back in two hours."

"Trust us, Tom-Tom," Dan drawled. "We're scientists now."

Laguna Pequeña beach was as crowded as always with local teenagers surfing, playing volleyball, and throwing Frisbees, but Tom and his friends managed to find an empty strip of sand to set up their tests.

"We'll test at twenty-five, fifty, and one hundred feet," said Tom. "I'll record my notes"—he held up his portable tape player—"and we'll use these playing cards instead of pencil and paper."

"Hey, mine are all clubs!" Dan complained.

"I've given each of you one suit of cards," Tom said, "but the suits don't matter. It's the numbers we're interested in. The sender will pick a card while his back is turned to the receiver. Then concentrate on the mental image of the card you picked, and the receiver will pick the card with the same number from his stack. Does everybody know what to do now? Okay, Rick and Dan will do the first test. Dan, you'll be the receiver."

Two hours later Tom had more information than he had set out to get. His friends drove him back to the lab, then stayed to hear the results of the test.

"The PT worked fine at one hundred feet, even two hundred," Tom reported, "but it did require the sender and receiver to remain in line of sight. No surprises there, but there *were* some surprises in some of the other results."

"Other results?" Mandy echoed. "I thought you were only testing for accuracy over distance."

Tom nodded. "That's what I thought, too, at first, but I started noting how many hits and misses each of you was scoring. Sandra and I have been batting a thousand since I recalibrated the receiver, so it hadn't occurred to me that it might be any different with other test subjects."

"Hey, you should have told me this was a competition," Rick said. "I would have tried harder to win."

"It's not a matter of winning or losing," Tom assured him. "But there are definite differences in how well each of you sends and receives." He picked up a pencil and jotted some notes and a graph on a piece of paper.

"What's all that?" Dan asked.

"If I break down your score results into three ranges, with one being least accurate and three being most accurate, this is what we come up with. Rick, you're a strong sender—a three."

"Numero uno, that's me," Rick quipped.

"But you're only a one as a receiver."

"I demand a recount!"

"Mandy receives in the three range with a perfect receiving score," Tom said, pointing to Mandy's portion of the graph, "but her accuracy as a sender is a two."

"Ouch. Second best. But I try harder."

"Good point. I think both sending thoughts clearly and receiving them clearly are skills that can be improved with practice. Which brings us to Dan."

"How'd I do, Professor?" Dan inquired.

"You're a three across the board, Dan my man. A perfect score at both sending and receiving. Who'd have guessed it?"

"Well, I would have, for one," Dan said, pretending to be hurt. "So what does all this mean in the real world?"

"Not a whole lot right now—unless, of course, you want to start practicing your mind-reading act in case the band never gets off the ground."

"Now I *am* hurt!" Dan exclaimed. "The Scavengers not become a major hit? How could you even *think* such a thing? We're planning a very impressive performance at Linda Brickowski's party Friday night—I think even you'll be impressed." He caught Mandy's eye. "Oops, I forgot. You won't be at the party."

Tom looked at Mandy, who seemed to be doing her best not to notice. "Well, maybe I'll be able to take an evening off by then. I'll just have to make up the time between now and Friday, I guess."

Mandy smiled at him. "Thanks, Tom. The party will be more fun if you're there, but I didn't want to say anything. I know how much your work means to you."

"My work *is* important, Mandy," Tom said, "but it's not my whole life. And I count on you not to let me forget that."

Mandy reached up and kissed him on the cheek. "You've got a deal, Swift," she said.

Two days later Dr. Weiss had his permission from the state of California to try his sonic liquefaction experiment, and Tom and Orb had the satellite link to the Global Positioning System up and running.

Teams from Swift Enterprises had peppered the fault line with portable digital monitoring devices. The devices used a second satellite link to send information back to the Swift Enterprises labs and from there to the computer in Los Angeles and SAM. Everything was ready for the big experiment that might avert a killer earthquake.

The plan called for Dr. Weiss and Mr. Swift to trigger the sonic cannons and monitor the results remotely from the Swift Enterprises complex. Tom postponed some fixes to the PT in order to be on hand when the results started coming through.

The atmosphere in the lab was tense but optimistic as Dr. Weiss flipped the switches that activated the six radio-controlled sonic cannons at the fault-line site. Mary and Hiroshi took positions at the consoles. Numbers began flashing across monitors, and dial needles swung wildly on consoles. Tom tried to keep track of what was going on, but a lot of it was totally unfamiliar to him.

"The cannons are up to operating temperature," said Mary, setting a series of dials. "Firing has commenced."

"One hundred feet," called Hiroshi. "Two hundred feet. Three hundred feet." The count went on as the supersonic emitters in the cannons fired a burst of sound into the solid rock of the fault. Digital seismograms poured out of printers, a march of numbers across a page. More technicians read them as they printed out. "Nothing yet," one of them reported.

"Fifty-five hundred feet," Hiroshi announced.

"Eric!" Mr. Swift shouted. "The temperature readings—look!" He pointed to a set of meters whose digital readings kept track of the internal temperature of the cannons. The displays were changing so fast it was difficult to read them, but Tom was certain the numbers were going up.

"Backup coolant system on-line!" Mary shouted. "Seven thousand feet!"

"Just hold out another four and a half miles," Dr. Weiss whispered, unconsciously crossing his fingers.

At just under two miles the temperatures began rising again, this time uncontrollably. The cannons slowed their descent as heat took its toll on their onboard systems, and one by one they stopped, miles short of their goal and irretrievably lost. There was silence in the lab.

"Eric, I'm so sorry," Mr. Swift said finally. "There must have been some flaw in the coolant system. We'll try again."

"How?" Dr. Weiss asked. "When?" He looked ten years older than he had an hour before. "Six of our eight cannons are two miles into the lithosphere. The remaining two won't help us now."

"They would if we could deliver them to the exact location where they'd do the most good," Tom mused.

"I suppose you have a delivery system that

will get them through six miles of solid rock without overheating them?" Dr. Weiss snapped at Tom.

"I might," Tom said.

Dr. Weiss glared at him. "I don't think this is any time for jokes, young man."

Before Tom could explain that he wasn't joking, a technician burst through the door with a sheaf of printouts. "Dr. Weiss!" she panted. "An emergency transmission from SAM!"

Dr. Weiss snatched the printouts from her hands and scanned them. His face went white. "It's worse than I thought," he said, sitting down hard in a chair. The printouts fell to the floor and fanned out in a jumble of unreadable numbers.

"What is?" Mr. Swift demanded. "What's wrong?"

"SAM reports that instead of easing shear stress on the fault, our experiment decreased some of the clamping stress instead. All we've done is move up the timetable for a killer quake. According to SAM's calculations, we can now expect 'the big one' within seven days!"

72

8

A STUNNED SILENCE FILLED THE SEISMOLOGY lab. The only sound for over a minute was the relentless ticking of the printers attached to the digital seismographs and the whisper of paper falling into catch trays. Tom could feel the fear and apprehension as he looked around the room. Finally Mr. Swift broke the silence.

"Well, Eric, what's our next step?"

Dr. Weiss shook himself like a man waking suddenly from sleep. "Outside of evacuating southern California, I'm not sure there is one," he said.

"Tom, do you have any suggestions?" Mr. Swift asked.

Dr. Weiss shot them an irritated look. "Really, I think this boy scientist thing has gone far enough, don't you? We're talking about the lives of tens of thousands of people, perhaps many more than that. Let the boy go back to his gimmicks and parlor tricks and let the real scientists handle this."

A look of anger crossed Mr. Swift's face. He started to reply to Dr. Weiss's outburst, but Tom put a hand on his father's shoulder. "It's all right, Dad," he said. "Dr. Weiss has been under a lot of stress. I'll just go on back to my lab."

Mr. Swift walked Tom out into the hallway. "Do you have a plan, Tom?"

"You've got two sonic cannons left, right?"

"Right, but they won't be enough for another test."

"Not another test like the one you ran today," Tom said. "But what if we took them all the way to the source of the trouble—slowly, so they don't overheat—and backed them up with some laser cannons?"

"How?"

"Mounted on the TANC. Of course it's going to need a few modifications." The TANC, or Transformable Ambulatory Nuclear-powered Craft, was an all-terrain vehicle, supersonic jet, and state-of-the-art spacecraft all in one. Tom figured that with some major retrofitting it could function just as well as an inner-earth rig to deliver Dr. Weiss's ultrasonic message where it was most needed.

A slow smile spread across Mr. Swift's features as he comprehended Tom's plan. "That's my boy," he said proudly. "I'm sending all the notes on this project to your lab and assigning you a crew of technicians. Eric may not know we need your help, but I do."

"Thanks, Dad. I never doubted that you believed in me. I'll get started right away," Tom said. "And thanks for the chance to help."

"You may turn out to be our only chance, Tom."

When he returned to his office, Mr. Swift contacted Harlan Ames for a briefing on their other problem—STAND's threat to further destabilize the quake zone. Harlan explained that law enforcement officials were searching everywhere for Edmond Audreys without success. He had apparently gone into hiding.

That afternoon Central Hills Police Chief Robin Montague and the Swifts' old friend Phil Radnor from the FBI visited the Swift Enterprises complex, where they found Tom and his father going over the latest improvements on the TANC.

"I just wanted to follow up on the investigation of the attempted plutonium theft last Saturday night," Phil said to Tom and Mr. Swift. "Could I have a look around the power plant?"

"Of course," Mr. Swift said. "Let's stop off and pick up Harlan on the way."

When they finished their tour of the crime scene, they returned to Harlan's office.

"We've questioned a number of rank-and-file STAND members," Phil Radnor told them, "including George Perry, who's currently in the Central Hills city jail. Most of them were cooperative, but we came away with very little useful information."

"I get the impression that they don't know any more about Audreys than we do," said Harlan, "and that isn't much."

"I understand you sent a private undercover agent to infiltrate one of their branch offices," Phil said.

"Jessie Gonzalez has obtained volunteer work in a local STAND office," Harlan said. "Tom has equipped her with a miniaturized camera, and this morning we received a telephone transmission of some digital photographs she took of people who've been coming and going there."

Harlan slipped a disk into his desktop computer and loaded the program that would show Jessie's pictures. The first face to appear on the screen was Rob's.

Phil frowned. "They have robots?" he asked.

"Uh, no, that's Rob," Tom said. "I took his picture to demonstrate how to use the camera. Sorry about that. The rest of the pictures ought to be a lot more useful."

The agent looked at the remaining eleven pictures, nodding from time to time. When all the photos had run, he turned to Mr. Swift. "Can you get me a copy of that file and the program that runs it?" he asked. "I recognize a couple of those faces, men with international connections."

"What are you getting at, Phil?" Mr. Swift asked.

"A few years ago the FBI and Interpol were closing in on a character by the name of Edwin Williams, a renegade CIA operative who was selling arms and explosives to terrorist groups all over the world."

"I read about that case," Tom said. "He died in an explosion a couple of years ago, didn't he?"

"*Someone* died," said Phil, "and not long afterward Edmond Audreys suddenly appears with a flimsy background and a bunch of criminal hired hands. He's about the same size and build as Williams, and the face could be plastic surgery. We haven't been able to get fingerprints yet—the guy wears gloves everywhere he goes, and he's apparently very accomplished in disguise, too. He slips through our best surveillance like a snake."

Yes, but there's more than one kind of fingerprint, Tom thought. And if a few more things fell into place in the next few days, he just might have a surprise for Phil and for Mr. Edmond Audreys.

"I'll take this file back and modem it to Washington," Phil said. "If there are outstanding warrants on any of these henchmen of his, we'll be able to make some arrests and maybe unearth some more details about Audreys and where we can find him."

"I hope so, Phil," Mr. Swift said. "Because this man is holding the state of California hostage."

"You know," Tom mused, "if it's true that Audreys is involved with terrorists—and he's sure been acting like one with that bomb threat of his—he could be waiting for the state to close the nuclear plants so that he can steal more plutonium before the state can transport it to safe storage."

"That's exactly what we're most worried about," said Phil. "The attempted theft at Swift Power was an inside job, but we think Audreys pulled off the others personally. That means he's already found his way into at least two operating plants under full security and come out with weapons-grade plutonium, and nobody's laid a finger on him."

"And if he has his way," added Harlan, "homemade nuclear devices could be in the hands of dozens of terrorist groups within weeks!"

On that grim note the meeting ended. Tom knew that time was running out, and much was left to be done. He hurried back to his lab.

By Friday afternoon work on the TANC was well under way. Tom designed modifications and handed them over to Rob and Orb, who were in charge of engineering and construction. The crew Mr. Swift had put at Tom's disposal was made up of hard workers with a great deal of mechanical knowledge and experience, and the modifications to the TANC were ahead of Tom's original schedule.

Mr. Swift had come by to check on the team's progress when Orb floated in and came to rest beside Tom. "You asked that I remind you to call Mandy and tell her you won't be attending the party tonight. This is your reminder." The basketball-size robot spun on its axis and floated into a workroom.

"Not going to the party, Tom? Why is that?"

"Oh, you know, Dad," Tom said, indicating their busy surroundings with a wave of his hand. "There's still so much to do."

"Now, listen here, Tom," his father said. "You've been putting in far too many hours on this job and getting too little rest and recreation. Do you honestly think you can give the TANC project your best when you're overworked and exhausted?"

"No, Dad, but—"

"And I know this was probably supposed to be a secret, but weren't you going to field-test the PT? I'm sure that project hasn't been getting much attention lately, with the earthquake scare and all."

Tom sighed. "You're right, Dad. It just

seemed so frivolous to be going to a party when there's so much in the balance—STAND and their nuke threat, Dr. Weiss's earthquake prediction, the TANC project . . ."

"You deserve some time with your friends," Mr. Swift said with a smile. "I'll see to it that Swift Enterprises doesn't come to a grinding halt while you're away."

Mr. and Mrs. Brickowski were away in Europe, so Linda and her older brother, Larry, had the run of the place. Tom wasn't sure that was such a good idea when he saw dozens of teenagers sitting around eating pizza on the furniture. The party was big, loud, and already starting to get rowdy when Tom and Mandy arrived with Rick and Sandra.

Larry Brickowski had just pulled in with half a dozen friends from college. They had a huge aluminum keg of beer, which they proceeded to haul upstairs to put in a bathtub of ice. "Hey, Swift, you and your pals want some of this?" Larry asked, hefting one end of the keg. "It'll be right upstairs and ice cold. Just follow me."

"Thanks anyway, Larry, but no thanks," Tom said. "We'll find other ways to entertain ourselves."

"Suit yourself, Swift," Larry said with a wide grin at his friends.

Larry Brickowski was Tom's idea of a total loser. His parents had enough money to send him to any college in the country, but his grades had sent him to Central Hills Community College, where he barely scraped by in his classes and spent most of his time playing poker and losing.

He owed a bad character called Philly Jarrett more money than he was going to be able to repay out of his allowance before the turn of the century, and it was beneath Larry to hold down a job.

Larry came back down the stairs and slapped Tom on the back. "Okay, so you don't want a beer. Let me show you something you *will* like."

"I'm not sure we'd be interested," said Tom.

"Nothing remotely illegal, Swift," Larry assured him. "But something you're all sure to enjoy. Follow me."

They followed Larry down the basement stairs to where a large set of double doors opened onto a huge game room filled with state-of-the-art electronic arcade games. "Feast your eyes and flex your fingers, guys. It's all yours."

"You boys go ahead," said Sandra. "I'd get bored with this in about two minutes flat. I think I'll find something else to do."

"You sure?" Rick asked, never taking his eyes from the incredible array of games.

Sandra laughed. "Absolutely. If I don't hear

from you in a week or so, I'll send a Saint Bernard with a cold soda."

Wandering through the big house, Sandra found a den, where Linda Brickowski and a bunch of kids were playing Pictionary. Sandra ran her fingers through her hair as she entered the room and suddenly remembered she was wearing the PT. It was so light and inconspicuous she had forgotten all about it. This might be an excellent place to try a field test.

She sat and watched the game for a few minutes, and when it was time for a new player, she clapped her hands to get everyone's attention. "I'd like to try an experiment," she said. "I'll bet I can read the mind of anyone in the room and draw the picture before she does."

This got a big laugh, but everyone was willing to try. Linda agreed to try first. "Think of a picture," said Sandra, "and look into my eyes. Wait until I'm done drawing, then draw the picture you were thinking of."

Linda looked at Sandra, who concentrated for a moment, then began drawing. "Okay," Sandra said when she was finished. "You can start drawing now."

Linda made a quick sketch, then they traded papers. "I don't believe it!" Linda said, astonished. "This is exactly what I drew!" Everyone gathered around to look, and their laughter turned to amazement.

"Who's next?" Sandra asked.

They had been playing Sandra's mind-reading game for about thirty minutes when Larry Brickowski came in with a beer in his fist. He went to stand on the other side of the room, where he watched the game intently. "Can you really read minds?" he asked her when he had watched half a dozen demonstrations.

"Yes," Sandra said, "but only when I'm wearing this." She moved her hair aside to show the ultraviolet transmitter just above her ear. "It's one of Tom's more interesting inventions," she said. "A psychotronic translator. It's on this little headband." Sandra took the PT off, and everyone gathered around to have a closer look except Larry, who stayed standing against the wall, a strange thoughtful look on his face.

When Sandra left the den, she noticed Larry following her. Rick and Tom were undoubtedly still hypnotized by video games, but Mandy would probably be somewhere else by now, so Sandra went looking for her. Larry might be harmless, but he made her feel nervous, and she didn't want to be walking through the house alone with him lurking around.

She found Mandy sifting through Linda's CDs for some music to play. "Which group should I put on?" Mandy asked her. Dan's band had already played one set, but the neighbors had called and complained about the noise.

"Take your pick," Sandra said. "I don't think anyone's listening at this point. I'm going to find a bathroom and fix my hair."

"I'll go with you," said Mandy.

In one of the Brickowskis' huge bathrooms, Sandra removed the PT headband and took a brush out of her handbag. "I wish Larry Brickowski would either pass out or just go away," she told Mandy. "I'm getting tired of his creepy looks."

"Well, maybe Tom and Rick will get tired of playing video games and we can get out of here early," said Mandy. "Or maybe we should just go down and drag them out of there."

"Now, *that's* the best idea I've heard tonight!" said Sandra.

Just then the door to the bathroom burst open, and Larry and one of his friends staggered in, waving a large rat by the tail. " 'Scuse me, ladies," he said, slurring his words a bit and weaving on his feet. "I caught this guy in the kitchen, and I was wondering if you had any idea what I could do with him." He waved the rat in Sandra's face.

"That's a rubber rat, Larry," she told him, anger making her voice tremble, "and it's still closer to being a human being than you are!" She rushed out of the bathroom, and Mandy followed. "That Larry Brickowski is such a loser," Sandra fumed, "and I don't mean just at poker!"

Larry smiled to himself as he picked up the psychotronic translator from the countertop. He held it high and regarded its reflection in the mirror. "Little buddy," he said, "you and me are going places!"

9

ON SATURDAY STAND ISSUED ANOTHER WARN-
ing. "The nuclear power plants are still in full
operation," Edmond Audreys said on his latest videotape. Seated in front of the TV set,
Tom noticed that the man's amused look was
gone, replaced by cold anger. "Evidently, the
state of California thinks STAND doesn't mean
business. I can assure you we do. We have a
nuclear device, and we will not hesitate to
explode it before midnight tonight if the
power plants are still operating." He gazed at
his unseen audience with unfeeling eyes that
sent a chill up Tom's spine. "You have been
warned."

The news reporter came back onscreen.
"State and local law enforcement officers

have scoured the area surrounding all the nuclear facilities but have found no trace of a bomb of any kind. Officials now believe that Audreys is simply attempting to terrify the state into shutting down the plants, and attempting to gain publicity for STAND, his antinuclear organization. The Swift Power facility has been closed, but the governor feels that closing the two state-owned plants would create a serious energy deficit."

"What do you think, Dad?" Tom asked, switching off the TV. "Do you agree there's no bomb?"

"All I can be certain of is that there's no bomb anywhere in this complex, including the power plant," Mr. Swift said, "and no way for anyone to get into the complex with the security measures Harlan's taken. If I felt any different, I'd evacuate the whole place, but Harlan and his teams have been over every inch of Swift Enterprises and a mile in any direction outside with every kind of bomb-sniffer you can imagine, including your own."

Tom had invented an explosives detector, based on olfactronic circuits he'd built into Rob, that sniffed out certain organic compounds found in conventional and plastic explosives even through a foot of concrete. Since conventional explosives would probably be used to trigger critical mass in a home-made atomic bomb, the Swift Enterprises security teams were using Tom's device as well as any others on hand, just to be on the safe side.

"All *I* know," said Tom, "is that when I look at that guy, I can't help thinking he'd do just about anything to get what he wants. My gut feeling is that human life doesn't mean very much to him."

"I'm afraid you may be right about that, son," said Mr. Swift.

"Tom, I think I—" Sandra began when she entered the lab.

"—misplaced the psychotronic translator," her brother completed the sentence.

"That's right, I—"

"—called Linda to see if you left it at the party, but she couldn't find it anywhere in the house."

Tom burst out laughing at the expression of amazement on his sister's face. He turned his head and pointed to the tiny flat button attached to the side of his head. "The next generation of PT technology, remember? Don't worry about it, just ask Linda to call when she finds it."

"Okay," Sandra replied. "I'd be surprised if she could find the major appliances in her house after that party. What a mess. I hope for Linda's sake the place looks normal by the time her parents get back."

"Well, I don't think she's going to be able to count on much help from Larry," Tom said.

"That guy is such a creep!" Sandra said. "He acted like a total jerk, and now Linda says he left sometime during the night, taking her good Raiders baseball cap. He *did* leave a note saying he'd return the cap."

"He'd better, if he knows what's good for him," Tom remarked. "Linda's pretty attached to that cap."

The intercom buzzed, and Mr. Swift's face appeared on the monitor. "I've got good news and bad news, Tom. The good news is, Eric's softening up a bit on the Terra-Tank idea."

Tom smiled at his father's casual use of the new name he'd given the TANC after modifying it for subterranean exploration. "Does that mean he's agreed to go on an expedition into the fault line?" Tom asked.

"No, but it means that he's no longer flatly refusing to discuss the matter," said his father.

"Well, it's a step in the right direction, anyway," Tom said with a sigh. "What's the bad news?"

"Jessie Gonzalez has pushed the panic button, and we've lost radio contact. I'll get back to you as soon as we know anything."

"She'll be all right," said Tom. "She can take care of herself." He wasn't sure if he believed it himself. He switched off the intercom.

"Oh, this package arrived for you," Sandra said, pulling a small padded envelope out of her pocket. "But there's no return address on it."

"I think I know who it's from," Tom said. He opened the package to reveal a necktie, still knotted, and a note from Jessie Gonzalez. "This was hanging on a coatrack in you-know-who's office," it said.

"Rob," Tom called to the robot, "give this a complete going over and log the olfactory components for a later match."

"Right away, boss," Rob said.

"What's that all about?" asked Sandra.

"I'll let you know later," Tom said.

"Okay, I guess. Oh, I forgot to mention that Rick is coming by soon to get me," said Sandra. "We're meeting Mandy and Dan at the beach. I don't suppose you'd like to come along?"

"Maybe I will at that," said Tom, eyeing some portable equipment on the workbench. "I have an idea for an afternoon's activity that might be fun."

An hour later Sandra was grumbling.

"Some fun," she complained, fitting the bulky headset over her hair and adjusting the large padded earpieces. "I just love to go to the beach and put giant contraptions on my head, don't you, Mandy?"

"It's not a contraption," Tom corrected her. "It's a testing device. Remember those hearing tests in grade school? It's a lot like that but designed to use sounds in much higher frequencies." He reached out and adjusted the headpiece to Sandra's head. "Hold up a finger if you hear anything."

Tom switched on the machine and began turning dials. Every couple of seconds he'd adjust a dial, then pause to see if Sandra reacted.

"Nothing yet," she said, shaking her head. Tom turned the dial again.

"Yowch!" Sandra screamed, ripping the headset away from her ears. "What was that?"

"That," Tom said, writing notes in his lab journal, "was a sound frequency your ears find quite unpleasant. Who's next?"

"You're kidding," Rick said. "You just made your sister screech like a wet cat, and you want us to try that thing?"

"Who're you calling a wet cat?" Sandra said, punching his arm.

"Ouch! Nobody! I don't know which of you Swifts is the more dangerous!"

"Okay, let me tell you the reason for all this," said Tom. "I'm planning to go with Dr. Weiss on an expedition into the earth's lithosphere in the TANC—excuse me, in the Terra-Tank. The objective is to alleviate some of the pressure on a certain portion of the San Andreas Fault that SAM, Dr. Weiss's expert system, thinks is ripe for an earthquake."

"The lithosphere, huh?" Dan said. "Are there any good hotels there?"

"I'm afraid I'll have to take my own hotel," said Tom. "The Terra-Tank will have life support for a trip of forty-eight hours: food, water, and air for three people."

"But you and Dr. Weiss are only two people," Rick pointed out.

"Now we know how he gets those great math grades," Mandy said, nodding knowingly.

"It's going to take three to get the job done," said Tom. "Me to pilot the Terra-Tank, Dr. Weiss to read the underground maps that will get us there and back, and a gunner to operate the sonic and laser cannons mounted on the outside of the tank."

"So why are you looking at us?" Rick asked innocently. "It's not like we've ever shared in these hazardous adventures of yours. I mean, would you let your friends get kidnapped by mad scientists with hordes of killer robots, or get dropped out of flying helicopters?"

"Or get attacked by giant prehistoric insects?" Mandy continued.

"Or be shrunk down to the size of ants?" Dan inquired.

"I think maybe they've got a point, Tom," Sandra said.

Tom remembered every one of those hair-raising adventures and close scrapes with a certain amount of fondness. After all, he and his friends had survived them and done a lot of good in the process.

"Okay, you guys, okay. I give up. I'd like to take you all, but only one of you can come along on the trip. I can't think of anybody I'd rather trust to help us get there and back again than one of you. But the Terra-Tank can't be completely shielded from the sound frequencies the sonic cannons use, and most people are pretty sensitive to them. Like Sandra, a minute ago. If I took Sandra into the lithosphere with me, her ears would never be able to take the punishment."

"So we all have to take the test?" Dan asked.

"Only if you want to, and the same goes for making the trip. I'll only accept volunteers. If none of you wants to go, I'll find a candidate somewhere at Swift Enterprises."

"Well, what can it hurt to take the test?" said Dan. "I'll go next."

Dan tested out fine to the highest frequencies the sonic cannons were capable of producing. Rick and Mandy were almost as sensitive as Sandra and were eliminated as candidates immediately.

"I guess I'm it," Dan said.

"What do you think, Dan?" Tom asked him. "Are you up for a voyage into inner space?"

"Am I!" said Dan. "When do we leave?"

"As soon as Dad can get Dr. Weiss warmed up to the idea. We think it's the only chance to avert the big earthquake he thinks is coming, but he's reluctant to try."

"Just let me know when you want to blast off, Captain," Dan said, giving Tom a mock salute. "Cadet Coster reporting for duty!"

"Say, isn't that Linda? Linda, over here!" called Mandy.

"Oh, hi!" Linda said, walking over to them. She looked distracted and worried. "Listen, I have something to tell you guys. Remember that gadget you left at the house, Sandra? Larry called. He's had it all along."

"Larry has the psychotronic translator?" Tom exclaimed. "What's he doing with it?"

"He says he went to an all-night poker game down in L.A.," Linda said. "That Philly Jarrett character was running it, and Larry wanted to use the PT thing to win back some of the money he owes before Philly has somebody break his arm or something."

"Oh, my gosh, and I let him get his hands on it!" Sandra wailed.

"It's not your fault, sis," said Tom. "So what happened at the poker game?"

"Well, he won. He won back all the money he owed Philly and some more besides. But when he tried to collect the money and leave, Philly said he'd been cheating and had one of his gorillas sit on him until he gave them the psycho-whoosis—he'd been hiding it under my Raiders cap!"

"You mean that now this lowlife gambler has Tom's psychotronic translator?" Mandy asked.

"Yes," Linda said, looking down at her feet. "And Larry said he was taking it to Las Vegas."

* * *

Audreys had said STAND would detonate the bomb at midnight on Saturday night. As that hour approached, the Swifts gathered together in the living room of their home, watching the TV for any news. A news bulletin came on, and everyone turned to the screen. "It is now just one hour until the time when Edmond Audreys of STAND claims he and his antinuclear group will detonate a nuclear explosive device near an operating nuclear power plant in southern California," said the reporter. "No such device has been found, and although large-scale evacuations of certain areas have taken place, authorities now believe that the entire incident is a hoax."

The studio graphic showed a picture of the Swift nuclear plant. "A member of STAND, George Perry, was recently arrested for the attempted theft of plutonium from Swift Enterprises' nuclear power plant. Although other, successful attempts have also been reported, there is no evidence directly linking the stolen plutonium to Audreys or STAND."

The reporter's features took on a grave expression. "Is Edmond Audreys bluffing? Or will California experience a nuclear attack at midnight tonight? No one knows."

"Oh, boy, another crisis." Sandra sighed. "This family sure knows how to have fun."

"Yeah, it's been a pretty strange week," Tom agreed. "First the earthquake, then someone tries to steal plutonium, then Audreys threatens to nuke California, Dr. Weiss's predictions, the fault-line test melts down, Larry steals the PT, someone steals the PT from Larry—I can't remember when I've had more fun!" By this time Tom and his sister were laughing so hard they had tears in their eyes.

"It pays to keep a sense of humor at times like this," their father agreed. "I just hope we're still laughing at midnight."

At two minutes past midnight the reporter from the earlier bulletin came back onscreen. This time his face was white and stricken. "We have just received a report that a small nuclear explosive device has been detonated underground in the desert near Santa Marina, California."

"I never doubted he'd do it if he actually had the bomb," said Mr. Swift, shaking his head sorrowfully.

"Due to the remote location," the reporter continued, "damage as minimal, and no loss of life has been reported, but there is some concern that the force of the explosion may have caused damage to the foundation of the nearby Santa Marina nuclear power plant. We'll have details on this startling story as it develops."

Mrs. Swift turned down the volume on the television. "Santa Marina is more than a hundred miles from our house," she said. "Do you think this area is safe?"

"I think so," said Mr. Swift. "Audreys himself said it was a low-yield device, and I think if it weren't he'd have bragged about it."

"Besides," Tom added, "if the device was buried far enough underground, there would be very little radioactive venting, if any."

Before anyone could respond, the phone rang. Mr. Swift answered it. "It's Eric Weiss," he said after a moment, then listened to the other man with a growing expression of apprehension. "I understand, Eric," he said. "Call Moss at CalTech and get him out of bed and over here. We have to convince him this is no false alarm!"

"What is it, Dad?" Tom asked when his father hung up the phone. "What did Dr. Weiss find out?"

"He's been waiting by his computer for a call-in from SAM. SAM has analyzed the effects of the underground nuke on the fault system and says southern California can expect at least a magnitude seven quake within twenty-four hours!"

No ONE GOT MUCH SLEEP THAT NIGHT. MRS.
Swift and Sandra made sure there was plenty
of stored food and water, since a major quake
could easily interrupt supplies of both, and
put new batteries in all the flashlights and
the portable radio. They gathered all the
emergency supplies into one room and took
inventory. "A magnitude seven quake," Mr.
Swift reminded them, "will be almost ten
times as strong as the last one. We should
expect some damage this time."

"We should draw the curtains and tape the
windows," Tom said.

"And let's wrap and store anything that
might fly around and cause injury," Mrs.
Swift added. "Sandra, will you stay and help
me secure the house?"

Tom and Mr. Swift went to the seismology lab to meet with Dr. Weiss and Dr. Randall Moss from CalTech. Dr. Moss had been a pioneer in the field of plate tectonics, and Tom had read a number of articles written by him during his recent research into earthquakes.

When Tom and his father arrived, they found that Dr. Weiss had already laid all of SAM's latest printouts on the conference table and was going over them with Dr. Moss. Dr. Weiss was so preoccupied, Tom noticed, he didn't even seem to mind Tom's presence at the meeting.

"I have a lot of respect for you as a scientist, Eric," Dr. Moss said after the discussion had begun, "and I think SAM will be a real breakthrough in predictive seismology when you get some of the bugs ironed out, but I'm not entirely sure you're not jumping the gun on this."

"I know SAM's right about this," Dr. Weiss insisted.

"But the modeling programs at the university haven't reached similar conclusions based on the same data," Dr. Moss argued. "Something could be wrong with the way SAM is arriving at its solutions."

"It's also possible that SAM's method of analyzing information is revealing relationships your modeling programs are missing," Dr. Weiss shot back. "I've been feeding SAM data from Swift Enterprises' digital broadband seismometers, and—"

"Meaning no disrespect to your outstanding reputation in the scientific community, Mr. Swift," Dr. Moss broke in, "but your new seismometers are nearly as untested as SAM."

"But SAM *did* predict last week's quake," Tom said.

"Yes, but it wasn't the first time a single quake has been predicted," said Dr. Moss. "A magnitude seven earthquake was successfully predicted in China in 1975, for instance. The trick is to keep doing it."

"And what if SAM has done that trick?" Mr. Swift asked. "If the prediction is accurate, convincing the California Office of Emergency Services to issue an earthquake preparedness bulletin could prevent considerable loss of life."

"I read about the Chinese quake," Tom said. "The government issued a warning a few hours before it struck, and tens of thousands of lives were saved. Wouldn't it be better to issue a warning, even if it turns out to be wrong?"

Dr. Moss sighed. "Your point is well taken, Tom," he said. "I remember almost thirty years ago when my theories on plate movement were considered rash and unfounded, too. Young scientists will always challenge their elders with new ideas and new ways of proving them." He smiled at Dr. Weiss. "And although I'd rather be right about this and have no earthquake at all, I can't take the chance that I might be wrong. I'll call Emergency Services and have them issue an alert. May I use your telephone, Mr. Swift?"

"Certainly," Mr. Swift said. "It's in the office next door. Right this way."

Dr. Weiss leaned back in his seat and closed his eyes. "I thought we weren't going to be able to convince him," he said. "And without him behind us, we'd never be able to convince the OES."

He sat forward again and looked at Tom. "I have you to thank for this, Tom," he said. "I'm very grateful you were here tonight."

"I think Dr. Moss would have come around, even without me," Tom said. "But I'm glad if I helped at all."

"I'd also like to apologize for the things I said in the seismology lab the other day."

"You were upset over the test," Tom said. "I understand."

"I was, but that's no excuse for rudeness, or for pigheadedness, either. Your father kept me up-to-date on your tank modifications and how you plan to use it. He had a lot of faith in it."

"But it's not too late," Tom said. "Couldn't we lessen the severity of this quake by using the Terra-Tank now?"

"No, the timing is too close. I think the best

thing we can do now is to get ready for what's coming."

Tom's father came back into the room. "I'm inviting all Swift Enterprises employees and their families to remain at the complex tomorrow," he said. "We're better equipped to ride out a quake than anyplace else in California. Tom, perhaps you'd like to call your friends and see if they and their families would like to join us."

"We always seem to get together for those special social occasions," Rick was saying to Tom, Sandra, Dan, and Mandy as they sat on blankets spread on the Swift complex lawn overlooking Central Hills. "You know—parties, beach picnics, earthquakes."

"Hey, why didn't I think of it before!" Dan lamented. "The Scavengers have played a few parties, but we've never had an earthquake gig. I should call the guys! We could run some extension cords for the amps and set up right over there—" The others pelted him with fruit and crackers until he gave up on the idea.

The entire complex area was dotted with groups of people sitting on the lawn well away from the buildings. More people waited inside the buildings of the Swift complex, and a few cars were still straggling up the road to the perimeter fence. The infirmary staff waited to transport any injuries.

As the sun sank low in the west, coloring

the sky a deep gold, conversations slowed and stopped, leaving each person alone with his or her own inner thoughts and fears. Sunrise and sunset were both probable times for earthquakes, statistically speaking, and that seemed to be the thought on everyone's mind.

Tom reminded himself that they were safer here than anyplace else they could be, but a part of his mind wanted to give in to the fear and tension. He held it in check.

"Look!" someone shouted. Tom turned his back on the sunset and followed a pointing finger to the east—the direction of the fault line. At the eastern horizon the sky lit up with eerie flashes of light like fireworks set off near the ground. The sky seemed to crackle with some sort of awful electricity. "Earthquake lights!" Tom said. He knew that these flashes of light, probably caused by wildly fluctuating electrical fields at the point of fracture, were often the immediate precursor of an earthquake. "It's coming," he said. "Brace yourselves!"

The ground reared up and knocked Tom off his feet. He fought his natural inclination to try to get back up again as the violent forces of the quake rolled through the earth under him, throwing him this way and that on the ground. He saw Sandra and his friends struggling to stay in one place with nothing to hang on to but the ground that was doing its best to hurl them off. He could tell they were afraid but determined not to panic. In spite of their best efforts, though, they were being separated by the motions of the earth—Dan and Tom were about twenty feet away from the rest of them now.

As he struggled to get his balance, an awful roaring sound, like an immense animal in pain, filled Tom's ears. Then came a loud crack like a lightning strike as the ground in front of him ripped itself apart, and a huge opening appeared in the earth. The ground on both sides of the chasm sloped sharply, and dirt and rocks began to cascade into it.

"Run!" Tom screamed to the people near the fissure. People scrambled to their feet as best they could and fled uphill, away from the widening crevice.

Tom turned and stood but was knocked off his feet again by Dan, who was sliding out of control toward the crack in the earth. As Dan passed him, Tom dived for him and grabbed his hand. Dan stopped a foot short of the crevice. "Hold on, Dan!" Tom shouted over the roaring of the earth. "Don't let go!"

Dan gripped Tom's hand hard. "I'm doing my best, old buddy," he said, fear rising in his voice. Tom was facing downward now, and as the ground tilted at a desperate angle toward the crack, he tried to dig in with his toes and his free hand to stop sliding. From far away, over the awful noise, he could hear someone calling his name.

Dan dug one foot into the broken earth and pushed himself another inch away from the crack as Tom pulled. "That's good, Dan!" Tom said. "Do it again!" Dan brought the other foot up and pushed, gaining another painful inch. Inch by inch they gained ground as rocks, shrubs, and picnic coolers tumbled past them to pitch into the yawning hole. "We're doing it!" Tom shouted. "Just a little bit more!"

The ground heaved again. Tom's feet lost their grip, and Dan's weight began pulling them both inexorably toward the open fissure. Just as Dan slid over the edge, Tom found a foothold.

Dan shouted and tightened his grip on Tom's hand. "I can't hold on, Tom," he said, his voice weak and frightened.

"I won't let you go, Dan," Tom assured him, but he knew he wouldn't be able to hold him forever. His arm and shoulder ached horribly, and his hand was beginning to grow numb. He could see people trying to reach them, but he didn't think they would get to him in time.

Tom took a deep breath and began to pull against Dan's weight, ignoring the pain in his arm. He willed all his strength into pulling, but the earth groaned again, and the fissure began to close up again. Tom watched in horror as the two sides of the rift came closer and closer together, with his friend trapped helplessly between them.

11

WITH A FLASH OF LIGHT ON METAL AND A strained creaking of earth, the gap began slowly to widen.

"Pull, Tom!" Dan cried. "I can't hold it much longer!"

Tom turned his head to see Rob, his wide metal feet and hands planted firmly in the walls of the crevice. He strained against the awful strength of the earth as it pushed the sides of the rift together. "Tom, hurry!" Rob urged.

Tom pulled with all his strength and with strength he didn't know he had. His arm felt as though it were on fire as Dan began to rise out of the crevice, inch by inch. His feet touched the edge and he flailed for footing, but the ground gave way beneath him. Tom gripped Dan's arm with both hands and with a grunt hurled himself backward in a last desperate attempt. They landed in a heap.

Breathing hard, Tom scrambled to his feet to see Rob stuck in the crevice. The silvery robot was still pushing against the crevice walls that were trying to crush him. "Rob!" Tom shouted. "Get out of there! Jump!"

Rob bent his knees and sprang straight upward, clearing the edge of the gap just as it smashed shut with a roar below him. He landed on the ground with a loud clanking noise. "We did it, boss!" Rob said, his beaming photoreceptors the only part of him not covered with clumps of earth.

As suddenly as it had started, the quake was over. There were a few seconds of terrifying silence, then the earth shuddered once and was still again. Tom helped Dan to his feet, and they crossed the place where the awful gap in the earth had been only moments before to rejoin the people on the other side.

Tom looked around and saw people, dazed by the violence and terror of the last few minutes, rising unsteadily to their feet. Those who had decided to ride out the quake inside were coming out of doors cautiously, as though unsure that it was really over. He waved to his family and his friends.

Mandy broke loose from the group and ran

up to Tom and Dan. She threw her arms around both of them, crying with relief. "We thought we'd lost you!" she said.

"I thought so, too," Dan said and fainted dead away. A stretcher crew came running and carried him into the infirmary.

"Now that we know Dan's all right, and we're all okay," Tom said to Sandra, Rick, and Mandy, "I'd like to go into Central Hills and help the emergency crews. The police will be busy keeping order, and the fire department will be plenty busy if there are any gas fires."

"Are you sure you feel up to this?" Mandy asked. She indicated the restraining sling that strapped Tom's left arm firmly to his side. "That arm's sprained pretty badly."

"I have to admit it hurts," Tom said, "but someone might need our help."

"I'm going, too," Mandy said.

"Count me in," said Rick. "I don't know anything about first aid, but I'll help any way I can."

"Me, too," said Sandra, "but we ought to let Mom and Dad know."

"Right," said Tom. "Let's all check with our folks, then meet at my van. Sandra had better drive."

"Wow, I think this is a first," Sandra said. "I ought to get you to sprain your arm more often."

Fifteen minutes later they were piled into Tom's van, heading for Central Hills. Sandra drove cautiously, mindful of possible road damage. Twice they had to ease over a drop of several inches in the pavement. In other places the road was displaced horizontally, with the center line divided half a foot between one piece of road and another. The glow of fires lit the horizon as they approached town, and a police roadblock greeted them at the city limits.

"I'm sorry," said a patrolman as he leaned in the driver-side window, "but we're asking that no one enter town. We have a state of emergency."

"Let them through, officer," a voice said from beyond the reach of their headlights. Tom peered into the shadows but couldn't see much. Then Chief Robin Montague stepped into the light and raised a hand in greeting. "These are responsible young people, and we can use their help," she said.

"Whatever you say, Chief," said the officer. He stepped back to let them pass.

Tom rolled down his window and leaned out. "What's it like in town, Chief?" he asked.

"Fortunately, we were somewhat ready for it because of the earthquake preparedness bulletin," said the chief, "but there's still quite a lot of damage, and a few people are still missing. I'm sending you to the Central

Oaks Apartments at the corner of Oak and Second. Do you know where that is?"

"Yes," Mandy said. "It's that brand-new apartment building."

"It was," Chief Montague replied. "Apparently, it wasn't built to quake code standards, and now it's a pile of rubble. A crew is there now excavating by hand—we believe there are several people still in the basement."

"Are they alive?" Sandra asked.

"We don't know yet," said the chief. "We can only hope. Pull your vehicle up to the crew and turn your high beams on—they're going to need all the light they can get. Someone there will direct you what to do next."

"We'll get right over," Tom promised.

"Thank you," Robin Montague said, her voice weary. "I wish we had a hundred more volunteers like you." She stepped aside and waved them through.

When they pulled into the parking lot at Oak and Second, Tom couldn't suppress a gasp of shock at what he saw—huge piles of rubble mounded on the ground beneath the building, whose east-facing wall had crumbled.

The contents of the apartments had been flung onto the ground outside by the quake, and some pieces of furniture and appliances teetered precariously on the naked edges of the ruined apartments. Over the clatter of tools Tom could hear an ominous creaking from the building itself.

Sandra pulled the van up to the work crew and left the headlights on. A man in a hard hat, covered with plaster dust from head to toe, came up to meet them. "Name's Bob," he said. "You here to help? Let's go, then." He walked away from the van, and they hurried to follow him.

"You'll need these," Bob said, handing them each a hard hat. "Here's what's happened. The first floor of this building has collapsed into the basement. There's a family name of Carson unaccounted for—Scott and Jane Carson and their kids, Danny and Lori. They live on that floor."

Tom and his friends looked at the devastation that had been the home of a hundred people only that afternoon.

"Maybe they're somewhere else," Tom suggested. "Somewhere safe."

"That's what we're hoping," Bob said, "because otherwise they're still in there somewhere. Until we know, we dig. We've got more tools than volunteers, so grab something and I'll show you what to do."

Bob kept talking as he headed toward the building. "The debris has to be cleared by hand. With heavy equipment the vibrations might cause the whole place to collapse on us, and then there are the aftershocks to worry about." He directed Tom, Sandra, Rick, and Mandy to a crew moving the rubble one agonizing piece at a time, using their hands and a few simple tools.

The work progressed slowly, but finally a section of splintered flooring gave way and crashed into the space below. White dust rose up from the hole.

"Hello!" Tom called. "Is anybody down there?" He put his ear to the hole and heard a tiny sound. "Did you hear that?" he yelled to the others. "Somebody's down there!"

"Don't get your hopes up," said one of the other volunteers. "It might only be the sound of the building settling. This whole thing could collapse any time."

"I'm going to have a look," Tom said. "The opening's big enough for me to squeeze through."

"I'll give you a hand," Rick offered. "You're short one." With Rick's help Tom eased into the hole and dropped down several feet onto the floor. The impact caused a flash of pain to shoot up from his feet, but he barely noticed it. Rick handed him down a lantern.

Tom walked across the floor, stirring up clouds of plaster dust. The lantern made a circle of yellowish light in the gloom as he played it around the wreckage. The building creaked above him. "Anybody down here?" he called again. "We're here to get you out!" This time he was certain he heard something—a voice coming from the other side of a pile of rubble just in front of him.

He ran back to the opening. "Rick! Mandy! Sandra! Get down here and bring a crowbar and a first-aid kit, quick!"

In moments his friends scrambled down. Working as quickly as they could, they pulled away chunks of wall and floor from the place where Tom had heard the voice. Every minute or so they stopped to listen. At last they could clearly hear a child's voice.

"We're stuck!" the child called. "Me and Lori are under this table, and we can't get out!"

"Are you Danny?" Tom asked.

"Uh-huh. Do you know where my mom and dad are?"

Tom swallowed hard. "No, Danny, I don't know where they are for sure, but let's get you and your sister out of there, and then we'll find them, okay?"

"Okay," the little boy said, his voice trembling. "Just hurry, 'cause Lori's scared."

"We're hurrying, Danny. Believe me, we're hurrying." Using the crowbar to loosen pieces that were jammed together, they moved the large chunks of debris one at a time. Tom unstrapped his injured arm and used it almost as much as his good one. Finally their lanterns showed a small opening to the room beyond.

Tom tore at the rubble with hands that were already starting to bleed. When he had a hole big enough to crawl through, he grabbed a lantern and started in. "Rick, stay out here in case we need help," he said.

Mandy and Sandra followed behind. "We're in the room now, Danny," Tom said. "We should have you out of there in a few minutes." He shone the lantern around the room. It showed a ghostly coating of plaster dust on everything. A dining table was barely visible in one corner, jammed between a refrigerator and several other pieces of furniture. Two people lay motionless on the floor a few feet from the table, partially covered by fallen chunks of the ceiling. A shattered ceiling beam pinned them down.

"Rick, get a stretcher crew down here right now!" Tom shouted. Mandy hurried over to the people and began checking for signs of life. Tom and Sandra pushed against the fallen refrigerator that blocked one side of the table. Slowly it began to move.

When they had moved the refrigerator two feet or so, Tom got down on his knees and looked underneath the table. Two children, perhaps four and six years old, were huddled underneath, eyes wide with fear. The boy had his arms around his sister, whose face was streaked with tears.

"It's all right now, Lori," Tom said. "You don't have to be afraid anymore."

"So then they took the parents to the emergency infirmary, and the doctor there said they're going to be just fine," Tom explained wearily. He was back home with his parents and Sandra. Most of the Swift employees and their families had left to assess the damage to their own homes. Dr. Weiss and Mary and Hiroshi were still correlating data and would probably work all night.

"That's wonderful news, Tom," Mrs. Swift said. "I'm very proud of you and Sandra for saving those people's lives."

"Oh, even if we hadn't been there, Mom, I'm sure someone would have found them," Sandra said.

"Maybe," her father said, "but it was you and your friends who made the difference."

Sandra got up from her chair. "I'm going to try to get some sleep in spite of the aftershocks," she said. "Could it be I'm actually getting used to nonstop earthquakes?"

"Don't get too used to them," Tom teased her as she left the room. Then he turned to his parents. "Why don't we see what the news is about the quake," he said, reaching for the remote control.

When the TV came on, he recognized the face of Dr. Randall Moss. Tom turned up the volume.

"The movement that occurred today along the San Andreas Fault, with a magnitude of seven point three, has almost certainly relieved most of the pressure that had been accumulating for so many years," Dr. Moss was saying. "I think we can look forward to peace and quiet along the fault line for a good many years to come."

Mr. Swift looked at his watch. "That reminds me, Tom. I promised Eric Weiss I'd come by the seismology lab and check up on SAM's latest findings. Would you like to come along?"

"Sure, Dad," Tom said. "Don't worry, Mom, I'll get plenty of rest tomorrow, now that the worst is over." But even as he spoke, Tom had serious doubts about the accuracy of his statement.

His fears were confirmed in the seismology lab.

"It's not over yet," Dr. Weiss said as he handed Mr. Swift a stack of printouts from SAM.

"So you don't agree with Dr. Moss's analysis that the stress has been relieved by the quake," Tom said.

Dr. Weiss took off his glasses and rubbed his eyes. "One of the most prevalent theories in traditional seismology is the Seismic Gap," he said. "It states that once stress on a fault has been relieved, it takes a long time for another major quake to strike that fault."

"Makes sense to me," Tom said, "but I'm an amateur."

"It makes sense to the professionals, too, which is why I believe they've been missing evidence to the contrary that's right under their noses. I have statistical evidence to prove that quakes are actually *more* likely to occur in areas believed to be safe according to the Seismic Gap theory."

"But why?" Tom asked, confused. "If the fault has moved, why would there still— Wait, I've got it! The lithosphere is as much as six miles deep, and if the fault doesn't move to the greatest depth . . ."

"Exactly," Dr. Weiss said. "There's still stress. If the quake isn't at least seven point five in magnitude, there's a good chance that the pressure on the fault, rather than being relieved, has simply been redistributed."

"But to where? The pressure has obviously been reduced at the point of fracture," Mr. Swift said.

"And redistributed to the ends of the fault segment," Dr. Weiss said, pulling down a map. "Here and here"—he pointed to spots north and south of the fracture—"are the next likely places for a quake to strike. While we might expect a quiet time of a few months or a few years, SAM says we won't be so lucky the next time. We can now expect a magnitude eight quake on the southern San Andreas."

"How long do we have?" Mr. Swift asked, his face grim.

Dr. Weiss looked down and shook his head. "Perhaps slightly more than forty-eight hours." Then he raised his eyes to Tom's. "We have no choice now but to take the Terra-Tank into the earth."

12

DAD, I THINK I KNOW HOW TO CAPTURE AU-
dreys," Tom said as he and his father headed
back to the Swift house to tell Mrs. Swift and
Sandra that Tom would be leaving at first
light.

Mr. Swift's eyebrows shot up. "I'm listening," he said.

"Well, first, we know what he's after," Tom
said.

"Plutonium," Mr. Swift said.

"Right. And his last attempt to get some
didn't exactly work out. So, what do you say
this time we make it easy for him?"

"What do you want to do," Mr. Swift said
with a chuckle, "invite him in to help himself?"

"Pretty much," Tom admitted. "You'll have

to do most of the work after Dr. Weiss and I leave—you and Harlan. Rob will help you out, too. Now, here's my plan. . . ."

With Dan pacing nervously next to him, Tom watched the sky lighten along the eastern horizon, then lowered his gaze to the Terra-Tank, which was poised to begin its journey deep inside the earth. Both sonic and laser cannons were pointed slightly downward, ready to make the first cut into the earth's surface that would start Tom and the others on their way down.

Dr. Weiss had insisted that he be the leader of the expedition, and Tom had agreed. Tom was relieved that the scientist's attitude toward him had undergone some changes, but Tom still had the feeling that Dr. Weiss regarded him as some kind of whiz-kid marvel rather than a working scientist in his own right. When Tom mentioned bringing along the psychotronic translator to run some terrestrial interference tests during the journey, Dr. Weiss had shaken his head in disgust and said, "Whatever you like, Tom. Just don't let it interfere with the real reason we're going down there."

Tom watched Dan and Dr. Weiss climb aboard the tank, looking awkward in their bulky, heat-resistant silver suits. The suits were a variation of the spacesuits Tom had designed for use aboard the Swift supershuttle. The advanced Swift design would provide protection against the extreme temperatures as the craft approached the asthenosphere, the region beneath the lithosphere where the high temperature made solid rock as soft as taffy. Even with the exceptional heat-shielding on the Terra-Tank, temperatures were expected to be uncomfortably high, and the suits contained onboard climate-control systems designed to keep the three terranauts from overheating.

"I'll understand if you want to change your mind, Dan," Tom told his friend as he entered the tank and prepared to seal the hatch. "This is the most dangerous thing I've ever done, and there's no guarantee any of us will make it back."

"You honestly think I'd miss being one of the first terranauts just because it's *extremely* life-threatening?" Dan asked. He shrugged his shoulders through the heavy fabric of the spacesuit, reached past Tom, and threw the bolt, sealing them in. "Well, I might at that if it weren't for you, Tom-Tom. If you designed this hunk of junk, then I believe it can get us where we're going and back in one piece." He patted a console affectionately.

"Well, I hope your confidence is justified," Tom said.

"Besides," Dan added, "you need me. How're you going to pilot and man the guns with one gimpy arm that you got by saving my life? I owe you one, bud."

Tom smiled and gave Dan a high-five with his good arm. Then he began to prepare for their descent.

Dr. Weiss was loading SAM's maps from a computer disk into the Terra-Tank's onboard computer. They would be displayed as bit-maps, and he would be able to enlarge any area for greater detail or call up another map on a moment's notice.

Tom had arranged for Orb to run communications from the seismology lab as long as radio contact was possible. Once they entered radio blackout, deep inside the earth's crust, no one would know their fate until they all appeared back on the surface—or didn't. The tank would support them with air for forty-eight hours, and Tom figured the trip down and back would take about thirty.

Tom, Mr. Swift, and several Swift Enterprises engineers, with help from Rob and Orb, had run a complete preflight check on all the craft systems to be certain that nothing had been left to chance.

"I don't want there to be the slightest possibility that this vehicle will fail to bring its crew back safely." Mr. Swift had said, his voice gruff with emotion. "So we'll check everything, and then check it again."

Another team had gone over the spacesuits and helmets, and a third had loaded the

Terra-Tank with supplies of food, water, and air.

"I'm sending along a supply of this special electrolyte-replacing fluid," Mr. Swift had said, showing Tom where on the Terra-Tank it was being stored. "If temperatures get higher than we expect down there, or if the heat shields and spacesuits don't operate as efficiently as we think they will, you'll suffer from dehydration and electrolyte loss. If that were to happen, you could easily collapse and be unable to operate the tank, so don't forget to drink this instead of water if it gets too hot."

"I won't forget, Dad. Thanks."

Dr. Weiss had set on the tank's dashboard a timer that would count down the time until SAM's estimation of the great quake. "I admit it's foolish," he'd said. "The quake could be hours before or after the forty-eight hour mark. That's why we must make the best possible time without endangering the cooling systems on the cannons."

Finally Mr. Swift had brought out a bottle of mineral water and proposed an official launching for luck. "I couldn't find any champagne on such short notice," he told Tom, "but I think it's the spirit of the occasion that matters." He'd handed the bottle to Tom. "Would you like to do the honors?"

Tom poised the bottle over the blunt nose of the tank and brought it down hard. "I name you Terra-Tank!" he said as the bottle shattered and sprayed him with cool water.

Tom remembered that moment now as the tank's engines gunned to life, its treads bit into the earth, and the craft pitched sharply downward.

They left the light behind, the opening they had made in the earth a shrinking disk of relative brightness that soon disappeared from their aft display. The four halogen lamps that Tom had mounted on the front of the Terra-Tank lit their way as the sonic and laser cannons chewed through solid rock like the jaws of a huge metal termite. They tunneled at the steady rate of a little less than one-half mile per hour. Tom piloted the craft, while Dr. Weiss consulted his maps and navigated, and Dan monitored the firing and internal temperatures of the cannons.

For safety they left their suits on, but Tom suggested they remove their helmets for comfort until they were needed. Dr. Weiss agreed. They doffed their helmets and concentrated on the mission as Weiss's "doomsday clock" counted down the time left before "the big one" leveled southern California.

Thomas Swift, Sr., picked up the phone that was buzzing insistently in his office. "Yes, this is Swift," he said. "Television and newspaper reporters? Anonymous phone tip? Sure, send them up. We'll be glad to give them a statement." He turned to Harlan Ames, who was seated in the chair opposite his desk. "This is it, Harlan."

"Didn't take 'em long to smell the blood in the water, did it?" Harlan said. He got up from his chair and opened the door to fifteen or twenty reporters, all eager to ask the first question.

"Mr. Ames, is it true you've resigned your job without notice?" one shouted over the others.

"Our tip said the reason was personal differences between you and Thomas Swift, the owner of Swift Enterprises," another voice called out.

"Is it true that most of the security staff is leaving with you? What effect will this have on Swift Enterprises?"

"Mr. Swift, last week someone tried to steal plutonium from your plant. With virtually no seasoned security personnel on hand at Swift Enterprises, wouldn't this make it a lot easier for you to be hit again, perhaps successfully this time?"

A television crew shot footage of the interview and more footage of Harlan and his staff leaving the Swift compound in plenty of time to make the evening news.

"Hey, Tom-Tom! When are we going to run those mind-reading tests you promised me?"

"Well, if you want, we can do one now and

124

one after we put the helmets back on the suits. Then we can compare the two to see if the suit helmet affects transmission."

Dr. Weiss snorted in disgust. "Honestly, this mind-reading joke has gone far enough," he said impatiently.

"But it's no joke, Dr. Weiss," Dan protested. Tom's test showed I was the best sender *and* the best receiver. I guess I'm just a natural mind reader."

"There is no such thing as thought transference, with or without Tom's little gadget, there," Dr. Weiss assured Dan. "There are, however, various tricks that a talented performer can use to make one *think* his mind is being read. I don't doubt that Tom is talented, but I wish he would devote more of his talent to solving genuine scientific problems and less to playing juvenile games."

"Let's can the test for now, Dan," Tom suggested. He realized that they were all beginning to feel the strain of the cramped quarters aboard the Terra-Tank, and he didn't want to antagonize Dr. Weiss unnecessarily. "How're we doing on depth?"

"Well, according to the old depth-meter on the wall, we— Hey! What's going on?" Dan exclaimed.

The tank stopped moving forward, though the cannons were still firing. Tom looked out the forward observation window into what seemed to be empty space. "Stop firing!" he called to Dan, who obediently flipped four switches. To Tom the silence seemed strange after the steady noise of forward progress they had been hearing for almost twelve hours.

Dr. Weiss walked forward, and the tank lurched violently. "Stay back!" Tom yelled, but it was too late. The tank pitched forward and turned over, end on end, falling through the underground space like a huge stone.

"Brace yourselves!" Tom shouted at the top of his lungs. "We're going to hit!"

13

A FEW MOMENTS LATER THE TANK CRASHED hard against the surface below, sending Dr. Weiss hurtling through the cabin. Tom, who was strapped in, grabbed Dr. Weiss and tried to reach between the scientist and the dashboard to cushion him from the worst of the blow. He felt a burst of horrible pain in his injured arm as Dr. Weiss slammed into it. Then everything went black.

The next thing he was aware of was Dan's voice echoing in his ears. "Tom! Tom, are you okay?"

"I think so," he managed. "Did we bring any aspirin?"

Dan peered at him anxiously. "Dr. Weiss is still out cold," he reported, "if anybody could be cold down here. I think he hit his head on the computer monitor. I broke out the first-aid kit."

Tom unstrapped himself and got slowly to his feet. The temperature in the tank felt quite warm but not dangerously so. Tom noticed that the floor of the cabin was tilted at an odd angle. He walked carefully to where Dr. Weiss lay unconscious, and Dan followed with the first-aid kit.

Tom knelt and felt Dr. Weiss's head for fractures. He couldn't detect any, but he felt a sizable lump where the scientist had struck the computer and found a cut that was bleeding profusely. Tom stopped the bleeding and dressed the cut, then applied a compress to keep the swelling down at the site of the wound.

"What happened to us, Tom?" Dan asked. "One minute we were standing still, and the next we were an unguided missile."

"We must have cut through to an existing tunnel," said Tom. "One that wasn't on Dr. Weiss's maps. My guess is we were teetering on the edge of a drop-off, and when Dr. Weiss came forward, his weight threw us off balance. We must have fallen at least a hundred feet straight down before we hit."

"This must be what it feels like to be in a car wreck," Dan said, rubbing the bruises his safety harness had left on his shoulders.

"I imagine," Tom said. "If it hadn't been

for our seat restraints, we'd probably be dead now."

Tom put a pillow under Dr. Weiss's head, and he and Dan got up to look out the observation window.

"Do we still have headlights, Dan?" Tom asked, peering into the gloom beyond the window.

"I'll find out," Dan replied. He flipped the switches on the halogens, but nothing happened. "It doesn't look good," he told Tom. "But I wore my glow-in-the-dark lucky socks, if that'll be any help."

"I'll keep it in mind for an emergency, Dan." Tom switched on various onboard systems to assess as much crash damage as he could without stepping outside.

"Hey, Tom?"

"Yes, Dan."

"I like to kid around as much as the next guy, but this is a real emergency, isn't it? I mean, are we totally hosed?"

"Maybe not totally," Tom said, "but both our front laser cannons and one of our sonic cannons don't respond to control. The lights you already know about, and the computer is completely shot."

"Now give me the good news," Dan said.

"We're alive, we're right-side up, and our life-support system is functioning at optimal levels."

"So we can stay alive down here another what, thirty-five hours?"

"Yes, but we're not going to sit around just staying alive," Tom said. "We're going to figure out how to get this thing back up to the surface."

Dr. Weiss stirred and moaned. "What happened? Where are we?" he asked weakly.

Tom and Dan hurried over to him. "We crashed," Dan told him.

"We're all right for now," Tom added, "but Dan and I are going to go outside and take a good look at the damage so we'll know how quickly we can be back on the road."

"Outside? But the heat—"

"Our spacesuits should protect us for quite some time, and they carry plenty of air, too. I added a small air lock to the Terra-Tank, so Dan and I will go out one at a time, and you'll be protected from the temperature out there."

Dr. Weiss put a hand up and felt the bandage on his head. "How long have I been out?" he asked.

"Only a few minutes," Tom replied. "How do you feel?"

"Awful. You grabbed me—kept me from flying around the cabin."

"Yes, but as you can see and feel, I wasn't one hundred percent successful," Tom said. "But I don't think there's any lasting damage, at least to your head. The computer wasn't so lucky."

Dr. Weiss sat up slowly and turned his head to look at the computer. "My maps!" he cried.

"I hope you memorized the route," Tom said. "We don't have the time or the components to fix the computer down here. We have to concentrate on getting the Terra-Tank moving and us to the surface before our air runs out. If we can find the right spot to exit to help the fault, so much the better."

"I understand," Dr. Weiss said. He took several deep breaths to clear his head and then began to help Tom and Dan with their helmets.

"I'll go out first and take the tool kit," Tom told Dan, checking the helmet seals on their spacesuits. "When you see the red light on the air lock go out and the green light come on, that means the outer door is closed and you can go into the lock."

"Red light, don't go," Dan repeated. "Green light go. Got it."

"When the inner door is secure, open the outer door, but don't step down until you've checked your footing. We don't know what it's like out there."

"You wearing the PT, Tom?" Dan asked.

"Yes, and we'll try it out. Now, just remember what I said."

"Red no, green yes. See you outside, Captain."

"Dr. Weiss will monitor us from the control

panel by watching the video feed from our suit cameras."

Then Tom stepped into the air lock and secured the inner door. Next he opened the outer one and looked out—there was solid rock below his feet. He stepped down onto the floor of an immense cavern. The rock walls were slightly luminescent, creating an eerie, underwater kind of light.

A few moments later Dan joined him outside. "Awesome!" he exclaimed.

"It sure is," Tom agreed. "Let's have a look around." Tom set down the tool kit and walked as far as he could go in the shortest direction. His helmet light shone on rough stone walls zigzagged with deep cuts and striations. He signaled Dr. Weiss on his suit radio.

"Yes, Tom?"

"Are you watching my video monitor on the control panel?" Tom asked him.

"Yes, I am. The cavern is quite impressive. This sort of formation sometimes happens when a large pocket of gas becomes trapped in molten rock. If the rock solidifies before the gas escapes, a chamber like this can be the result."

"I don't think that's what happened here, though," said Tom. He stepped closer to the nearest wall so that Dr. Weiss could see the crisscross pattern incised into the stone. "Have you ever seen anything like this?"

Dr. Weiss was stunned into silence for a moment, then his voice came over Tom's radio. "I don't think anyone has ever seen anything like this before, Tom. I can't imagine what forces could be responsible for such a pattern."

"Maybe we can get some samples while we're here," Tom said. "Then you can figure it out when we get back upstairs."

"Maybe you'd better come have a look at our ride, Tom," said Dan, who had wandered back over to the tank. "It doesn't look real good."

Tom walked around the tank once, checking for damage. "It looks as if we've got our work cut out for us, Dan," he said with a sigh. The heat-shielding had held, though there were hairline fractures, but there didn't appear to be any serious structural damage.

As Tom suspected, the steel cages protecting the halogen headlamps had been caved in and the lamps themselves shattered by the impact. One sonic cannon had broken off the body of the tank and lay in pieces on the cavern floor. The other was not damaged, but both laser cannons were pretty banged up.

"I don't know how much help I'm going to be with this arm," Tom said. "It's worse since the crash. It hurts so much I think it might be dislocated."

"You do the thinking, Captain," Dan said with a mock salute. "I'll do the work."

133

As Tom came around one corner of the tank, a movement off to one side caught his eye. He turned his head, but nothing was there. "Did you see that?" he asked Dan.

"See what, Captain?"

"Nothing, I guess."

"Must be the heat," Dan said.

"Is your suit climate holding up all right?" Tom asked him.

"Just fine. A little warm but not bad. How about you?"

"Mine's working fine. Dad will be happy to hear the suits are testing out," Tom said with a smile, "not to mention NASA." A flicker of motion. "There it is again!" Tom turned to look, and this time in his helmet light he saw something white disappearing into a hallway off the main cavern.

"I definitely saw something that time," Tom said. "Dan, hold very still for a minute and let's see if it comes back."

Tom stood quietly and watched the spot where he had seen the white thing disappear. A minute later it was back, shuffling out of the darkness into the circle of light cast by his helmet light.

"It looks like some kind of mole!" Tom exclaimed.

"Yeah," Dan agreed, "but it's as big as a Rottweiler!"

"Dr. Weiss, are you getting a look at this?" Tom asked over the radio.

"Yes, but I don't think I believe it," the scientist said hoarsely. "See if you can get any closer."

"*You* can get as close as you want," Dan said. "I'm staying right here, thanks."

"Dan, uncouple one of the rear laser cannons so we can mount it on the front," Tom said. "Dr. Weiss, set up to record what I'm sending. I'll see if I can get some good pictures for you."

Tom stepped forward, one deliberate, slow step at a time. He kept his light trained on the creature, hoping Dr. Weiss was getting a clear picture. "It looks as if it weighs about seventy-five pounds," Tom said quietly. "It's a bit molelike in appearance, but instead of having fur it's covered with a system of overlapping plates of some sort of hard chitinous material, like living armor. Its front feet end in shiny white claws perhaps a foot long, possibly made of the same material as the armor plates."

"What about eyes?" Dr. Weiss said into the radio. "Does it have eyes?"

Tom looked closer. The animal's odd, blunt face featured some sort of mouth and a nose with bristly white whiskers, but where eyes would have been on a surface animal, there were only shallow depressions in the skull, covered by tough-looking white hide. "No," he reported. "No eyes, but vestiges of eyes. I

135

think these creatures may have evolved from a surface species."

There was a crash from behind him, and Tom turned to see Dan standing over the spilled tool kit. When Tom turned back around, the mole creature was nowhere in sight. "It has to have gone down this corridor in front of me," Tom said. "I'm going to follow it."

Guided by the small searchlight attached to his helmet, Tom walked down the narrow corridor in the direction he thought the creature had taken. It had left no prints on the hard rock, but Tom could see no side tunnels off this one. From somewhere nearby he could hear a repetitive scraping sound.

The tunnel in the rock grew narrower and shorter, and Tom had to squeeze just a little to get through the next few feet. If it gets any smaller, he thought, I'll have to turn back. There was a bend in the way, then the tunnel opened up into a wider room with a tall ceiling and more tunnel entrances higher up.

He heard the scratching again, right behind him, and turned to see at least twelve of the giant mole creatures, half again as large as the first, blocking his only way out. He backed slowly up against the rock wall as the creatures shuffled closer and closer, flexing their giant claws.

14

TOM! WHAT SHOULD I DO?" DAN STOOD AT THE doorway to the smaller cavern behind the mole creatures, who seemed to take no notice of him.

"Nothing yet," Tom said in as calm a voice as he could manage. "Radio Dr. Weiss, and don't shout or make any sudden moves, okay?"

"He's already on his way," Dan reported. "He suited up as soon as you took off after that thing. He's bringing that laser cannon I took off the tank."

"I don't want to hurt them," Tom said, eyeing the advancing beasts cautiously. "Not if I don't have to, anyway. I wish I could make them understand we're not here to hurt them."

"You can!" Dan said, tapping the side of his helmet. "You've got the PT."

Tom felt weak with relief. How could he have forgotten? He remembered how easy it had been to read Mickey's thoughts when the big black cat had participated in his early experiments. Since then the psychotronic translator had undergone a lot of readjustment to human brain patterns. Would it still work on an animal? Tom knew he had to find out—and quickly.

Tom faced the largest of the mole creatures and filled his mind with thoughts of peace and friendship. He sent a clear mental picture of himself and the animal talking together cordially while the other mole creatures watched quietly.

This won't work, Tom thought. I've got to turn my head slightly so that the PT beam can get beyond my helmet. But I designed this to work through the retina, and these creatures have no eyes! But if they're truly descended from some kind of surface mole, they may still have vestigial optic nerves near their eye spots. I'll aim for those and hope for the best.

To be on the safe side, he sent a verbal message, too: "We are peaceful beings who wish only to be your friends." It seemed to work—at least the creatures had stopped advancing.

Dr. Weiss appeared in the corridor opening and pushed Dan aside. "Hold on, Tom!" he shouted. He held the laser cannon in both arms. Tom's train of thought was broken, and the mole things began moving forward again.

"Dr. Weiss, put that thing down and be very quiet," Tom said calmly. "I'm trying to communicate with them."

"Communicate! How? Tom, you don't mean that mind-reading gag! This is no time for pranks!"

Tom sighed. He was trying to keep his thoughts calm and peaceful, but Dr. Weiss wasn't making it easy. "Dan, help Dr. Weiss set the cannon down as quietly as possible, then both of you stay right where you are. Be very quiet and don't make a move unless I call for help."

Dan and Dr. Weiss wrestled the heavy cannon to the ground and stood watching Tom and the mole creatures.

We are friendly, peaceful beings who wish you no harm, Tom thought at the biggest creature.

What are, question? Us are not! came the thought from the hulking beast in front of him. Tom felt a jolt of pure excitement. He had communicated with it, and it was intelligent!

"It says we're not like them. It wants to know what we are," Tom called to the others. *We come from above, from outside*, Tom thought at it.

Outside, story told to children is! thought the mole leader. *Us, the People are. This one, Pathway Finder is.*

139

Of course, thought Tom, they thought of themselves as the People. Any people's name for themselves could be translated that way, and the moles had probably never met another intelligent race. The name Pathway Finder probably meant that this mole was their leader. *I am Tom*, he thought, and wished he could remember what Thomas meant. *I am a friend to Pathway Finder.*

What are, question? Food are not, came the next thought.

Well, at least that last part was comforting, thought Tom. "It's name is Pathway Finder. I think it's the leader of the creatures. It doesn't believe we're really from the surface," Tom said. "Apparently, they no longer believe in the surface, though the idea still exists in stories."

"You could show them mental pictures," Dan suggested.

"I don't know if they have any way to process them," Tom said. "They must have been sightless for hundreds of generations. I'll have to try something else."

Tom crouched down to make himself smaller and less threatening. He made sure the beam would clear his helmet, then he closed his eyes and concentrated. He imagined cool wind on his face, damp grass under bare feet, the sound of birds and running water, the smell of a rose, the taste of lemonade.

Pathway Finder grunted and moved back a

step. *Us are not!* he thought at Tom. *But also rival are not I think. Hurt not, agree question?*

No, we're not going to hurt you, Tom thought. *Even though we're strange and different.* He held out a gloved hand, and the mole leader leaned forward to touch it with its whiskered nose.

The mole creatures backed away from Tom, all except for Pathway Finder, who shuffled up very close and touched Tom's hand again. *Outside true thing is question?* it asked.

True thing, sent Tom. *I will tell you more, if you want.*

Want, came the thought. *All must know. All will be here soon.*

"I don't know how you did it, Tom," Dr. Weiss said on the way back to the tank, but you managed to communicate something to them—I could tell by their actions."

Tom shook his head and sighed. "For the last time, Dr. Weiss, I've invented a device that encodes thought impulses on an electron beam and sends them from one mind to another. You don't have to believe me, but you just saw a demonstration of it."

"That could have been the same sort of communication one would have with a strange dog," Dr. Weiss retorted. "All I saw was that it stopped acting aggressive and seemed to accept you."

"Well, take it from me, these creatures are

a lot more intelligent than dogs. They're self-aware," said Tom, "able to conceive of themselves as beings separate from other beings. They're fascinated by us and by my descriptions of Outside. They're coming to the big cavern in a little while and bringing every member of their group."

"I'm sorry, Tom," Dr. Weiss said. "I have a great deal of respect for your scientific abilities, but I'm afraid you're deluding yourself about these mole things. At any rate, our primary concern now is to make our repairs and get away from here before the fault moves."

"And before our air runs out," added Tom.

"We started out with forty-eight hours of air," said Dan, who was hard at work on the critical repairs the Terra-Tank would need to begin tunneling again. "What do you figure we've got left?"

"Twelve hours from the launch to the fall," said Tom. "That leaves thirty-six. We gained three hours by falling instead of tunneling that last stretch but lost a lot more on account of repair time." He handed Dan a wrench.

"But the repair time is coming from suit air," Tom said. He saw Dan struggling with a bolt and realized he'd given him the wrong size wrench. "Here, Dan, try this one," he said as he handed him the next size up. "So we save tank air and use up suit air, which is good unless we need to use our suits on the trip back. They're intended as a backup system to the tank's climate control, you know."

"True, but the climate control's working," Dan argued. "So anyway, we have thirty-six hours of onboard air less the nine and a half hours we've already put into repairs. That's more than twenty-six hours for a fifteen-hour trip."

"Wrong on three counts, Dan. First, Dr. Weiss has been breathing cabin air most of the time we've been on suit air. Second, there's some loss through the air lock every time we go in and out. Third, the trip back would have taken fifteen hours with both sonic cannons firing at full strength. We're going to be limping along on one sickly sonic cannon and two crippled lasers. And," he added, "repairs aren't finished yet."

"Gee, I feel so much better now that you've explained everything," Dan said.

After Tom, Dan, and Dr. Weiss had gotten a few hours of much-needed sleep, the mole creatures came back as they had told Tom they would. Looking through the forward porthole, Tom saw hundreds of them, including many smaller, immature individuals who clustered excitedly around their elders.

"Dr. Weiss, look!" Dan shouted. "They're here, just as Tom said!"

Dr. Weiss looked through the porthole and stood silent, eyes wide. Finally he said, "I'm sorry, Tom. You were right about them, and I was wrong."

Tom came up behind him and put his hand on the older man's shoulder. "Let's go outside and meet our fans, Dr. Weiss—I have a treat in store for you." He opened his kit and removed two flat objects the size of shirt buttons. He handed one to Dan and attached one to Dr. Weiss's temple. "Remember to turn your head slightly so that the beam is directed at the creature you're communicating with," he said. "The PT operates on line of sight. Shall we go?"

Tom, Dan, and Dr. Weiss climbed out of the tank and soon were seated on the ground with mole creatures gathered around them. "Maybe you should ask them some questions about the fault system at this level, Dr. Weiss," Tom suggested. "It's probably as familiar to them as our backyards are to us."

"Good idea, Tom," Dr. Weiss said. "If we can tunnel directly to the most effective place to relieve the fault stress, it could make all the difference."

Dan was seated in front of a half circle of young moles, who seemed to be paying rapt attention to his every thought. Now and then one of them would raise a hind foot and slap the rock surface with it a few times, then wriggle in what Tom could only imagine was delight. Dr. Weiss was in a deep discussion with Pathway Finder about the lay of the land six miles down.

Tom felt a nudge against his hand. He looked down to see another group of moles gathered around him. *Outside, more about tell request,* one of them thought at Tom. He obliged with more sense-pictures of life on the surface.

"Tom! They know a perfect place to tunnel! You were right," Dr. Weiss said. "They know every inch of the fault system, and they know the earthquake is coming."

Worldshake comes and safe place-to we dig, Pathway Finder thought to Tom.

"They dug all this," Dr. Weiss said, indicating the huge cavern. "That's the explanation for the cuts in the rock! Their claws are incredibly hard—almost like diamond. And the rock at this level is softer than at the surface."

"Well, ask for the starting point, angle, and direction we should start tunneling, and let's get started," Tom said reluctantly. "I hate to say goodbye to our new friends, but we can't afford for our air to run out."

"Or our time," Dr. Weiss said.

"I have a feeling we've just become legends," Tom said as the Terra-Tank left the cavern of the mole creatures behind.

"You're right, Tom," said Dr. Weiss. "Those creatures will be telling their children about us for generations."

"Did you know they have music?" Dan asked. "They play a rhythm on the ground with their feet. I told them about rock 'n' roll." He smiled with satisfaction. "I don't think things are ever going to be the same down here."

When they had arrived at the spot described to Dr. Weiss by Pathway Finder, they changed angles and prepared for their rise to the surface. "Directly behind us is a magma chamber," Dr. Weiss said. "We need to weaken the wall of rock between it and us, then make a tunnel for the magma to rise into."

"Since that will also be the tunnel we're escaping through, we'll have to be careful not to weaken it too much," Tom said, "or we'll arrive back on the surface medium-well done. Dan, fire the remaining rear laser cannon as we move forward from here. Just fifteen seconds—I hope that's enough."

"I hope it's not too much," Dan said, readying the laser controls.

They slept most of the way back to the surface with the cannon on automatic firing. Tom woke from the heat, groggy, his head splitting from lack of oxygen. "Wake up!" he called to the others. "Something's wrong!"

"The temperature in here's a hundred and twelve degrees!" Dan reported. "And rising!"

"It's our heat shielding," Dr. Weiss said. "It's failing. Our air will be burned up by the heat!"

"And that's not all," Tom said, pointing at the rear display, which showed a river of molten rock was advancing on them, glowing like fire. "Dan, fire all forward cannon at maximum power!"

Tom stumbled to the compartment where Mr. Swift had stored the special electrolyte fluid. He brought a case of it forward and handed bottles to Dan and Dr. Weiss. "There may not be enough suit air to get us all the way up," he told him. "Drinking this will keep us hydrated. When you finish one bottle, start on another. We're not far from the surface now—all we have to do is keep ahead of that molten rock!"

"Climb, baby, climb!" Dan shouted as he watched the cannon chew their way into the wall of rock in front of them. It was clear the magma was gaining on them, but if they could keep any lead at all long enough for the tank to break the surface, they'd be safe.

"We're almost there," Tom said. "Only a few thousand feet more."

"Coolant system failure in the sonic cannon!" Dan shouted.

Tom punched a row of buttons and shot Dan a questioning look.

Dan checked the readings, gave Tom a thumbs-up sign, and said, "Backup system on-line. Hold out just a little longer." Then, pointing at the rear display, he yelled, "We're losing the race! Here it comes!"

Just then the Terra-Tank shattered through the surface of the earth, cannons firing at thin air. Dan shut the firing controls down as they raced across the surface. The magma bubbled up behind them, flowing over the desert like burning water, slowing as the cooler air began to solidify it. The earth shrugged, buffeting the tank and its occupants.

Tom smiled at Dr. Weiss. "We got back," he said. "I wasn't sure we would."

Dr. Weiss clasped Tom's shoulder weakly. "You did it, Tom," he said.

The tank rolled to a stop a few hundred feet from the Swift camp, where dozens of people were racing out to meet it. Dan came out first, followed by Dr. Weiss. "Where's Tom? Is Tom all right?" called Mr. Swift as he ran toward the tank. A dark-haired man in police uniform raced ahead of him and arrived first.

"I'm fine!" Tom called from the doorway of the tank and stepped out to face the barrel of a gun.

"NOBODY MOVE!" SAID THE UNIFORMED MAN, who leveled a machine pistol at Tom's head. "The whiz kid's coming with me, and so is all the plutonium in the fissionable materials safe at Swift Power!" He gripped Tom's neck in the crook of his arm and spun around to face the horrified crowd, his back against the solid protection of the Terra-Tank.

Tom tilted his head to allow himself to see his attacker. With the last strength he possessed, he sent a mental image of an onrushing wave of yellow-hot magma. The man jumped, startled, and raised the gun.

"I'll take that, Mr. Audreys," said a voice from above him, and a massive metal hand seized the gun and crushed it into scrap metal.

Audreys started to flee, but the metal hand struck the back of his head and knocked him to the ground. Several police officers rushed up and quickly handcuffed him.

Rob jumped down from the roof of the Terra-Tank and joined the gathering of people around Tom that included Mr. and Mrs. Swift, Sandra, Rick, and Mandy. "I hope you weren't too frightened, Tom," the robot said. "I wasn't going to let him hurt you, but I wanted him to incriminate himself. That way the case will be easier for the state to prosecute."

"Remind me to limit your access to the law library," Tom said, leaning against his father for support as they headed toward the waiting ambulances. Dan and Dr. Weiss were already inside one of the vehicles, awaiting transport to Central Hills Hospital to be checked out after their ordeal. "Of course you knew who he was all the time?" Tom asked Rob.

"Of course. He couldn't hide from his own chemical signature. After I processed the olfactory components on that necktie you gave me, all I had to do was wait around for a match, and bingo! He showed up with some real police officers earlier tonight. Will I get to testify?"

"I don't doubt it," Tom said.

Mandy waited by the ambulance door as

Tom was loaded inside. "Would it be all right if I rode along?" she asked.

"I thought you'd never ask," Tom replied with a smile.

Harlan Ames's face peeked around the doorway to the Swifts' living room. "Ready for visitors?" he inquired.

"I'd better be," Tom replied. "I think half of Central Hills is on its way to see me this afternoon."

"In that case," Harlan said, leading in Jessie Gonzalez, "I'd like to introduce you to my new assistant chief of security."

Tom held out a hand and Jessie shook it. "Congratulations," he told her. "I'm glad you're back safe."

"Well, I told you Harlan and I had a plan," Jessie reminded him. "If I suspected the STAND people were onto me, I was to head for his fishing cabin near Yosemite. He made me memorize the directions." She laughed. "I think I could still find the place in my sleep."

"After Harlan and I pulled off that phony resignation for the press," Mr. Swift said, coming in and taking a seat in his favorite chair, "he headed up there, hoping she'd made it."

"Speaking of the press," Tom said, "you guys fooled them pretty well."

"The important thing," said Mr. Swift, "is that we fooled Edmond Audreys, or should I say Edwin Williams. Audreys turned out to be the renegade CIA agent operating under an assumed identity. I'd say the FBI has an open-and-shut case on him this time. And he didn't do any lasting damage with that bomb of his, either. The bedrock underpinning of Santa Marina has stabilized. The power plants will all be back up and running within the week."

A slight tremor shook the house. Sandra, coming in from the kitchen with some snacks for Tom, almost dropped the tray. "Forget what I said the other day," she said, handing it over to her brother. "I'm never going to get used to earthquakes."

"Well, maybe you won't have to," Tom told her. "According to Dr. Weiss, SAM's latest analysis shows that all's quiet on the southern end of the fault."

"You and Dan and Dr. Weiss had quite an adventure," said Mr. Swift. "You went deeper into the earth than anyone's ever gone before and brought back evidence of another intelligent species sharing the planet with us."

"That's the most exciting part of all," Tom agreed. "If we ever mount an expedition to study Pathway Finder's people, I want to be a part of it."

Later that day Tom was in the middle of a group of his friends, telling of his subterranean adventures for what seemed to be the hundredth time.

"Enough of this," he said with a sigh. "I want to know what's been happening on the surface."

He turned to Linda Brickowski and asked, "Did Larry ever bring the psychotronic translator back from Las Vegas?"

Linda squirmed and looked at her feet. "Not exactly," she replied.

"Well, it's obsolete," Tom said, "but it does work in a limited way, and I'd hate to see it in the wrong hands."

"Oh, I don't think there's much danger of that," said Rick.

"Then we have it back? I don't understand what's going on here." Tom looked at the others, who suddenly found other things they were very interested in. "Tom, phone call for you!" his mother called from upstairs.

Tom picked up the phone. "This is Tom Swift. Yes, Chief Montague, I'm fine, thank you. Dan's here, and Dr. Weiss is back at work already. The psychotronic translator? Evidence in Philly Jarrett's fraud trial? Of course I understand. No problem, Chief— thanks for calling."

Tom hung up and looked at Sandra and his friends. "I think you guys have a story to tell me," he said.

"I had nothing to do with it, Tom," Linda said. "Dan, let's go get a cold soda out of the refrigerator, and you can tell me all about your adventure."

"You bet!" Dan said, following her to the kitchen.

"I'm waiting," Tom said after Dan and Linda had walked away.

"Well, we had to do *something*," said Sandra.

"So we went to Las Vegas," Rick continued.

"We'd searched Larry's room and found the address where Jarrett runs his game," Mandy added. "We disguised Rick with a wig and some dark glasses and got him into the game while we waited outside with the van running."

"*My* van?" Tom yelped.

"Well, you said I could drive it," Sandra explained. "Besides, it was the only car we could all fit into that would make it to Las Vegas without croaking in the desert."

"You're forgetting the best part," Rick said. "So then I pulled out my handy dime-store police badge and told them all they were under arrest. When Jarrett put his hands up, I pulled off his hat, snatched the PT, and lit out of there like there were tigers on my tail."

"We made a sensational getaway in the van, and the rest is history," Mandy finished.

Tom shook his head. "I can't tell you how sorry I am that I missed all this, but maybe it's for the best. I never would have been able to keep a straight face."

"So did you really save Tom's life?" Linda said to Dan as they rejoined the others. "Dan, you're so brave!" She felt a bicep appreciatively. "And so strong, too! Why don't we go over to my house for a while, and you can tell me more about how you single-handedly saved the whole expedition!" She led him out of the room by one arm.

Dan turned at the door and shrugged apologetically. "I can't help it if she thinks I'm the greatest thing since crunchy peanut butter," he said.

Tom burst out laughing as the door shut behind them.

"What's so funny, Tom?" Rick asked. "If you ask me, Dan made quite an impression on Linda."

"The only thing that impresses Linda about Dan," said Tom, "is the fact that he's breathing." He took off the PT button and held it up for them to see. "She just wants someone to clean up the mess from the party before her parents get home!"

Tom's next adventure:

Tom has just completed a supersecret project in the Swift laboratories: the creation of a powerful force field capable of protecting all types of vehicles, both on earth and in space. Now he's taken the device one step further. He has adapted it for personal use into an invisible shield that can deflect almost any attack—from bullets to electric bolts to laser beams.

But there's one power to which even the force field is vulnerable: the cunning of an evil genius seeking the perfect cover for his global crime schemes. He has seized the prototype, and Tom knows he must find a way to penetrate and destroy his own shield before the villain begins mass production and mass destruction . . . in Tom Swift #13, *Quantum Force*.